D1571168

The River Road

A Story of Abraham Lincoln

THE MERIDEL LE SUEUR WILDERNESS BOOK SERIES

the River Road

A Story of Abraham Lincoln

❖ ❖ DISCARDED

BY MERIDEL LE SUEUR

Woodcuts by Susan Kiefer Hughes

HOLY COW! PRESS
DULUTH, MINNESOTA
1991

Cover woodcut and all woodcuts ©1991 by Susan Kiefer Hughes.

Photograph of Meridel Le Sueur by Judy Olausen.

ISBN 0-930100-37-9
Library of Congress Number: 89-45543

Typsetting and design by MacNifique Publishing Services (Minneapolis, MN); printed and bound by Edwards Brothers (Ann Arbor, MI).

First Printing, 1991

Publisher's Address: Distributor's Address:

Holy Cow! Press   The Talman Company, Inc.
Post Office Box 3170   150 Fifth Avenue
Mount Royal Station   New York, NY 10011
Duluth, MN 55803

Library of Congress Cataloging-in-Publication Data

Le Sueur, Meridel
    The river road : a story of Abraham Lincoln / Meridel Le Sueur ;
woodcuts by Susan Kiefer Hughes.
        p.   cm. -- (Meridel Le Sueur wilderness book series)
    Summary : Recounts seventeen-year-old Abraham Lincoln's hazardous
raft trip down the Mississippi River to New Orleans to sell provisions.
    1. Lincoln, Abraham, 1809–1865--Journeys--Mississippi River-
-Juvenile literature. 2. Presidents--United States--Biography-
-Juvenile literature. 3. Mississippi River--Description and travel-
-Juvenile literature. 4. Slavery--United States--Juvenile
literature. [1. Lincoln, Abraham, 1809-1865. 2. Presidents.]
I. Hughes, Susan Kiefer, ill. II. Title. III. Series: Le Sueur,
Meridel. Wilderness book series.
E457.905.L39 1991
973.7'092--dc20
[B]   89-45543
                                                      CIP
                                                       AC

This project is supported in part by a grant from the National Endowment for the Arts in Washington, DC, a Federal agency.

For my grandmother MARY LUCY

and my grandfather MARK LUCY

from the Illinois county,

pioneers of Democracy,

for the people's Road in the Wilderness.

The River Road

A Story of Abraham Lincoln

CHAPTER 1

IT WAS LATE in the fall in the new state of Indiana, in the year 1828, and this boy I am going to tell you about had just slammed the lean-to door on his pa's yellow dog to keep him from barking. He could see the light come dim from the single window his step-mother, Sarah Bush, had put in since she had married his pa. His own ma had only a greased paper over a hole in the wall.

This boy I am telling you about could just write his name—Abraham Lincoln—and he had read three books, although he was nigh on eighteen years old. He wore a buckskin shirt, and drove a horse hitched to a bull-tongue plow of wood, and he said he had attended school only by littles. He was a tall, lonesome boy in the frost of the year, and his mouth

was stained by walnut meat and frosted pawpaws. A tall one, between man and boy, he stood on the fringe of the forest on Pigeon Creek in Indiana, on the rim of the cabin clearing. He had helped his pa build the log house when Nancy Hanks, his ma, was still alive and singing—*Skip to My Lou, My Darling*. He had just slammed the door to the lean-to for he didn't want them to hear the yellow dog howling at him. He wanted to be gone from there.

He was going to be gone by winter. He would not spend another winter in that cabin, eighteen by twenty feet, which now held thirteen people, all sleeping and snoring mightily. Sarah Bush, his step-mother, had brought three children by another marriage from Kentucky, when his pa had gone on the trek there to find a mother for his children after Nancy Hanks lay on the path of the deer, silent forever. One of them had married Abe's cousin, Dennis Hanks, and had a new baby, and they too lived in the cabin, sleeping in the corner on a bear rug.

Abe was telling himself he was going to leave, fly the coop, high-tail it through the tall timber.

Let Sarah Bush build him a loft, and whitewash the whole inside of the cabin and make him homespun breeches of thistle, and fight with his pa to send him to school. He would not stay. Winter was coming fast; the panthers were screaming; and the wolves began to close in on Gentryville. Soon the river would be frozen over; and the roads blocked by high snows; and he would be locked in again. Planting time would come, and by law his pa had him locked there till he was twenty-one, for every son by law had to help his father till he was of age to pay back for his borning. Then the forests would be clogged; and he would never get to chew the fat at Jones store in Gentryville. He would have to chop firewood day and night to keep out the creeping cold; his axe blade would be smoking hot; and he would plunge into drifts after the buried limbs and haul them out with chains. He would have to watch the children with colds and worms, and be on hand when they got lost, and drunkards froze, and cows got the trembles. Perhaps the dread milk sick would strike again as it had that awful winter killing his Aunt and Uncle Sparrow and Nancy Hanks.

And he hated his father. He had no right. That very afternoon, when they were shucking corn in the field by the Pigeon, Abe had been sitting on the rail fence. An ox caravan was slowly going by. On every wagon seat sat men and women who knew things Abe wanted and hankered to know. With questions he split open their craniums like trees, and looked inside, and they told him many things—about the town of Boston, for instance, and the new steam engines, and the spinning jennies, and news from Europe. He was shouting out to a high-spired, bearded, laughing man who leaned out of the wagon to answer when Tom Lincoln, his pa, came up from behind him and did an awful thing. He knocked him off the fence onto the ground.

That's what he did. Abe found himself sprawling on the ground. He had to get up in anger and humiliation, dust off his skinned knees and call out pleasantries to the questions asked by the caravan, and go

back with his pa and shuck corn. Tom Lincoln saw
no sense to learning. It buttered no parsnips, drew no
water, made no fire, paid no mortgages. He was agin'
it. Abe told him—the things I want to know are in
books. My best friend is the man who'll give me a
book I ain't read. But his pa had knocked him off the
fence in front of those eastern people.

His pa would be inside that crowded cabin looking
at the marks made with a burnt poker on the rafter
which showed how much he owed Grigsby and
Gentry, the only two gentlemen in those parts with
cash to loan. He would be growing sore as a winter
bear. He was a hardworking farmer, hunter, woodsman; but he never could get hold of any cash. Abe
often said laughing, his dad taught him to work but
didn't teach him to love it; and that he didn't love
work half as much as his pay which was never much.

He was a boy who felt very lonesome on a frosty
November evening in a lonesome country. The dogs
howled; the panthers cried; and he knew that his
stepmother, Sarah Bush Lincoln, would be listening
for him to bring that water down for the morning's
gruel. She could and would never get him to call her
Ma—not him—only one to be called Ma was Nancy
Hanks, dead of the milk sick, buried on the hill a

short spring and a long time away on the ridge. The spring cardinals would flash red in the thickets, and the deer would come down to the spring, and far down in the grass on her grave the crickets would cry, and the tiny blue flowers spring from her eyes. Now his sister Sarah was dead too, after she married one of the Grigsbys and had a baby who died with her.

Let his new ma put in a puncheon floor, make them change clothes once a week, and wash before spring, he would pay her no mind, except to bring her the water from the spring a mile away. She was already pressing for them to dig a well—nothing good enough for her and her brood.

Well, he set the water down a ways from the door. She would see it come morning. But almost at the same time Sarah opened the door and he was angry at her uncanny knowing always of his thoughts, his whereabouts, his sprouting intentions. He felt the forest back of him, the dark ring, always there no matter how you swung the mighty axe day in, day out, until your shoulders and back ached and the trees went down before you—the wilderness was always there, at your back, or ahead of you.

The light spilled out of the cabin as she opened the door. She had a dish of fat burning in her hand

that reflected on her plain, strong face. Abe felt a
pang for her alone in the cabin—no escape for her,
not ever.

She put her hand to her brow trying to see, feeling
him there. He could have run, but something in the
lonely figure of his stepmother kept him from it. He
felt his neck tighten as he thought of Nancy standing in that doorway, smaller, tenser, stranger than
Sarah Bush. But the voice calling him was the voice
of the new stepmother his father had brought back
from Kentucky, with all her young fry, and furniture,
and dishes.

"Abe—Abe—" she called, and her voice asked
questions of him and even grieved his going, and he
had not even told her yet. "Is that you Abe—son?"
He started toward her, but his father's bellowing
voice stopped him. "Abe—Abe Linkern, you no-
account, lean, lanky, lazy, booktotin' idjut, bring that
water to yore ma or I'll split a hickory on ye even if
you be over six foot in yore nekkid feet. You hear me,
Abe Linkern?"

She turned and told him to stop. He appeared in
the door bent with the "trembles." He bellowed into
the darkness. "You aimin' to set out ain't you, Abe? I
heerd it. You better not do that or I'll hev the law on

ye. No stone'll hide you, no river carry you out. I'll
see that you get yore comeuppance. Abe, you har
me?"

"Yes, Pa," Abe said to the lighted figures in the
door which he could see clearly. "I hear but I ain't a
child no more. This ain't my home place no more."

"Oh, Abe," his pa said, and Abe heard the plead-
ing of a lonely man, "this is yore home. Ain't you cut
every log here? Where else is yore home?"

"I don't rightly know," Abe said to the grave of his
ma. "I'm a wanderer," he said. "Time is agoin'."

They all stood in the wilderness night unable to
make each other understand. "Is Dennis home?"
Abe asked to break the heavy silence, "I'll go down
to the Jones store, I'll fetch him back, ma'm."

"Abe—Abe," she called after him, but he was
gone.

It was a mile and a half to the Jones store where
the blacksmith, the farmers, the lawyers would all be
gathering since harvest was over, and the circuit
court adjourned. There would be discussion, crack-
er-barrel argumentation, stories, laughter and jokyness, light and warmth of men holding out the bitter
wilderness night, building a man barricade against
the loss, the death and loneliness.

As he jogged down toward Gentryville he thought of himself, like a tree that has not been used. What was his beam strength? What his bending quality? What warmth would he give when lighted—what resistance when struck? What would be the strength of his heartwood? A willow is one thing, a pine another, and a hickory still another. A hickory endwise can stand a weight of nine thousand pounds. Like a tree, the seed of a man is carried over time, by wind, bird, or animal, is planted, grows rings, shows the good and bad years; the sapwood turns to heartwood, the green center hardens. He had heard a tree cry out when the axe struck deep into the heart.

Would he, Abe Lincoln, be cut down in the years of his sapwood?

He began to run toward the store, toward warmth and light and other men.

CHAPTER 2

HE WANTED to get as far as he could from the log cabin he and his pa and Dennis had built with Nancy Hanks, weaving and singing as they worked. Now another woman lived there with her kids and kaboodle, with a window and a door, while his own poor ma had no floor, no door, no window. They had hacked out six acres the first winter, stumps, roots, and pea vines. It was no good to paint the walls white as his stepmother had done; nor make a loft where he could read nights; and homespun pants were no good; and never mind all her ways to keep him there chopping wood, hoeing corn, planting and working from can't see to can't see.

But now before the first snow, before the white geese flew over; before the river froze; he would leave, high-tail it down the river, hotfoot it down the forest.

His trails had been a fifty-mile path around Pigeon Creek—nine miles to school when there was school, a jog trot to the mill with the corn or wheat to grind, so many hours to Axel Dorsey's, teacher, treasurer, where the first courts were held; down to the Ohio where he sometimes ran a ferry for Crawford; back to Gentryville where he sometimes kept store for Jones; and over to Grigsby's where he was field hand, chore boy, and baby-sitter for Mrs. Grigsby. Grigsby and Gentry were the only ones with money. He had his own secret paths to the best trees he had blazed for his raft, a trail to his dead mother's grave, and outlooks and studies where he went to be alone, away from jest and woodsman's tale, and work.

He sometimes got the Louisville paper at the store and read. It was the year when the Erie Canal opened up, and an oxcart train went through with thousands of books bound for the colony of New Harmony, where men came from Europe to find a new way to live together. The first railroad was running in Massachusetts and a long, tall, lonesome boy in Indiana had written on the front cover of the Columbian Class Book—Abe Lincoln, 1828.

In other books loaned to him he read about Henry Clay, a boy of the slashes, poor farmer, who rode like himself to the mill with the com. And Daniel Webster made speeches Abe read. And Old Hickory Jackson was running for President and Abe read that he, like himself, was born naked in the wilderness, had lived on acorns, and slept in the rain.

He strode on his long legs through the evening brush toward the river and the rhythm of his stride struck in his head and heart. His feet rustled in the dead leaves and the big-antlered trees lifted above him and rubbed their limbs in the cold wind. He loved the trees when they were without leaves; the struggle with the wind showed, and the years of drouth.

He stood on the ridge and saw the Ohio that day, and saw the ships going down the Mississippi to the Gulf where the boats of the world were harbored. He would hear great tales from strange men, and see vast libraries and the readers and the writers of libraries, and hear the big talkers of the day and see the newspapers every day. He could, yes, he could even sail around the Gulf east or west and never return to the graves on the ridge, to the misery of his father, and the suffering of his people.

His father had no right to hit him off the fence and he would not spend another winter in that cabin. One would surely die. There were always some who did not survive the winters.

He heard men talking and saw the glow of a small campfire. He knew the paths like a fox, and like a fox he passed freely on paths of his own, and knew the hidden dangers of a fallen tree, or a buried cave like a river man knows the river. He crept up without a sound, without turning a leaf and, standing behind a great cottonwood, he saw in a small clearing three fierce and bearded men, river thieves, and they were counting out pieces of money—one for you, and one for you, and one for me. Abe watched them, but counting money is very boring, and he crept back because it is also dangerous to interrupt men who love money. He went up the rise and stood in the cold, naked woods, and he felt that he might be cut down like the saplings he had cut for his raft, still green, to make a bow for an arrow, a handle for a basket for a purpose not his own.

He put his hands to the thin prow of his chest which seemed like a ship full of gnawings and fears like rats, and also hopes and longings he could not name—to *know*—to *read*—to *see* what other men were doing, to push back that horizon now sinking to the west into darkness with his own axe hands. He could wrestle any boy or man in Gentryville. He had written three papers—one on national politics, one on cruelty to animals, and one on temperance. He had read about three books and peered into others. He had a copy book in which he did sums, and he had written on the flyleaf:

Abraham Lincoln
His hand and pen.
He will be good, but
God knows when.

He had written for an Indian friend who died:

Here lies poor Johnny Kongapod.
Have mercy on him, gracious God,
As he would do if he was God
And you were Johnny Kongapod.

His mind worried and shook and dug down into the question of education, of learning. Here I am, he thought, hemmed in by poor land. Pa will lose what he has. The poor man's got only land and children.

My family are low, poor whites. He had thoughts of being a lawyer, maybe, like Mr. Breckenridge, not have to swing an axe, or be like he was an indentured slave bound to his pa till he was twenty-one.

He had heard and knew about the mechanics, farmers, river men, roustabouts, wanderers, exiles who had fought in the American Revolution. He knew the names of Clay and Jefferson and Patrick Henry—"Give me liberty or give me death." In Europe he knew the new people had risen against kings, shoved them out, taking pages from our Declaration of Independence. He had burst into campfires, and asked strange men questions, and he had pieced together many things.

He kept running and running. All America was running, running west. There were depressions back in the eastern cities, he had heard men tell of them; and new machines put men out of old trades; and free land was stretching west. Jefferson had bought a big hunk of it, and there it lay now, and what was to become of it? He shook when he thought of the prairies he had heard men speak of—a vast empire. What would men do with it?

He did not know what to do. Most likely Dennis and Allen Gentry and the others were whooping it up at the Jones store by now, but he always felt embarrassed before he got into company; after the ice was broken, he hid his gawkiness by telling stories, winning laughter. He was afraid of girls. He did not want to marry. He kept running, loping along. Someone cried out—"Who goes thar?" But he didn't answer or stop. A horse whinnied from the darkness; a dog barked as he skirted a cabin. He saw old Grundy's empty cabin; they had gone west into Illinois.

He had loped along quite a while before he realized someone or something was following him. It was not a crash, nor even any kind of noise. It was a feeling. The long light was fading away even on the ground, thick with leaves as long evening fell to the west.

When he stood and listened, it stood also, and he could feel it listen for him as he listened for it. The hackles of his neck rose, and he knew he was being followed by a beast more silent than himself. He did not hurry. He kept a steady pace and once he turned and saw eyes in the darkness, and picked up a cudgel and began beating the side of a tree. For a little while the beast did not follow, and then he knew it was coming again—a panther. He kept running and striking the trees. At last the panther left him, took a path of its own.

The path rose to the crest—to his mother's grave. The far cry of the wolves spoke of winter. He came to the grove, and the cleared place of his mother's grave where in spring the little blue flowers would grow and he would be gone. Buried without bell or book, she lay in the path of the deer whose tiny feet she always liked to hear dancing in the winter snow, or the young fawns springing in the summer air with the cardinal's song and the red buds blooming.

"Where shall I go? What am I on this mortal coil? We all die to rise no more. Mammy, what can I do, where can I go. It is cold. It is lonesome."

He let the soft earth comfort him, and the damp rot of fall leaves was a good smell.

He must have fallen asleep. He thought he heard her call. "Abe . . . Abe, my dear son, Abe." He was shouting into the deep darkness, bellowing "Ma—Ma—" and his cheeks were wet, and he cried in the stillness, alone, with no eye watching him.

CHAPTER 3

IN THE DARKNESS, unseen by man, only by the small-eyed creatures with their own melancholy in the forest, he talked to her in the wilderness, and let his grief pour out in the fall darkness with the cold biting like sharp fox teeth, the brown nuts drying and falling, and the graves silent and sweet in the wild plum thickets. The summer like a golden cup had been poured out and now he felt empty and naked like the great boughs of the trees he loved.

He thought he heard her calling in the wind, as she called him at night, out of the thicket of his loneliness—"Abe—Abe, Abe, my little shirt-tailed wilderness baby." And he could see her in the thicket ahead of him laughing, her mouth stained by berries or parched by persimmons. They had a game

21

they always played— "Where are you from? Where do you live? In a sieve."

"In a sieve," he cried, "that's where I live, in a sieve." He remembered her sayings—how she had told him men grow like acorns, the scar at the butt end, and you press it down into the earth and it becomes the root of the infant king of the forest. Spring rains warm, the embryo stirs, two hands of the praying leaves unfold, reach out, take hold on soil and darkness, and the enduring span has begun in acorn or man; and how the young sapling grows, with no pith, no tissue at first, filled with water, and every summer makes the heartwood grow, a light and broad band for each year—and slowly, slowly, the sapwood turns to heartwood—slow in a man as in a tree, and the bending strength is made, and the bearing strength, and the straightness of the grain, what warmth he will give, and how he will turn to the uses of his fellows.

That was what she said.

In the long nights when they were alone, in the slow and many summers, she told him, "Your life is like a tree, its soil is the people, the roots go down. Your body lives on the body of all, long drawing of strength and nourishment from the strengths of time." Now he felt he reached down with some tap-root and took the strength of his mother.

She had said once, "Dead wood loves the fire. . . . You can hear the rich salt cracking. I love to hear it. It's like salt to the ear." A strange thing to say.

He saw now she was a working woman, a forest-walking woman, digging, bending, rising, hoeing, birthing. He saw always little pictures of her in the forest, standing under the crab apple trees at Sinking Springs in Kentucky, near the big pikes. Teaching him to write his name, A-B-E; bringing in teachers from the pike and asking the questions for him till he learned to ask his own. The work they did together was always different than any he would ever do again. She had a quick jokyness, and a different song for the hoeing, planting, berrying, soapmaking, spinning, carding, canning, shelling, and grinding, skinning, tanning. They all had their songs and sometimes their dances.

This is what she told him. "We are the great common, the very pore." She was tall and stooped a little, and always when her hands were busy, unlike a man, she talked. She had deep tree-bole eyes like he had, and a high forehead she tried to cover with hair, for people said—bad enough for a woman to know how to read without looking like she could. She had gray eyes like his own and flecks of beyond in them. "Abe," she said, "yore like me. You got eyes seeing beyond."

Standing with the deer at the spring mouth he saw her, laughing, beckoning, her dark treebole eyes looking into him, her eyes often sad, indrawn. He saw her sitting on the old nag when they came on the Kentucky side down to the Ohio, and she said the river Jordan must look like this, bright and shining. And when she had seen the new land no better than the old, she had lifted her skirts and sung *Skip to My Lou, My Darling*, until they all were laughing.

And Abe thought of the short years there, and how he brought the water for her a mile from the spring, and chopped the wood for the cooking in the three-faced cabin where they spent the coldest winter he would ever see. But she had many a story to tell to forget the cold as they ground the cold corn with pot and pestle. He could hear her laughter under the ground and her hands clapping as she cried at the shining waters of death—"It's the river Jordan for sure, and we'll all cross over." She was a believer in God and the Bible, but mostly in mankind, in work, foundations and strong roofs, good and kind rivers, everyday washing, patching, fixing, scrubbing, along with dancing and singing which the church did not always like. "It's the common doings," she said, "that hold the face of God."

That is what she said. So he had gotten her a preacher to spell her across that river, and he had said with the spring cardinals flashing red and the little flowers eager to come up—"Be ye comforted. In my father's house are many mansions . . . ." And he knew she would cross over into valleys of song and meadows of plenty—over yonder, as she was always saying. She had crossed the river Jordan for sure and he could see her looking back at the hills of Indiana and Kentucky, beckoning to him—calling him.

"Oh Mammy, Mammy," he cried into the dark earth that would soon be frozen solid, but he'd be gone.

CHAPTER 4

ABE THRUST OPEN the door to the Jones store. It banged back and every man there looked up to see a gaunt, dirty-faced scarecrow, who looked like a man, but had the gangly look of a boy to him, as if he wasn't used to being so tall, reaching so far so soon, standing so high.

Abe saw his cousin, Dennis Hanks, by the cracker barrel, McSweeney, the Irish school-teacher, Grigsby and Crawford, his bosses, and old man Gentry and his young son, Allen. The Kentucky attorney, Mr. Breckenridge, had just said, "Let the South keep their slaves . . . ." Every man jack of them saw Abe wipe his dirty face with his sleeve, and a kind of terror came in the door out of the wilderness night, and they saw he had been crying.

Abe saw a look of fear cross their faces and knew they felt the loneliness, the fear of unknown country, and the hard toil and now winter coming on. He shut the door and closed out the wilderness night and everyone began to talk at once as they no longer heard the baying of the dogs, the cry of the panther, the fall of dying leaves on the ridges, and the step of the little foxes holing up for winter.

"Howdy, Abe!" they all cried. "Howdy, Abe Lincoln. Well, Abe, how is it up there, how's the weather up there?"—a stale joke he learned to grin and bear to keep from socking the joker. "How is it, boy?" they all cried. "Will we last the winter? Will we keep our land—what will happen to us? Can you see us down here? His pa taught him to work, but he says he never taught him to love hit! He ain't much fer work but can he tear through one of them books!"

Allen Gentry, Abe's age, a pale youth who was going to school (and his pa would give him a good, fat farm, and he would marry the best girl in Gentryville), piped up, "I watched him working fer my pa cutting posts and I barely could see him moving!"

Old Grigsby, Abe called Blue Nose, patted his little fat stomach. "Abe ain't much fer work."

"And you ain't much fer payin' fer work," Abe said, and they all laughed.

"Why," said Mr. Crawford, getting himself a pinch of snuff (he owned the ferry Abe worked on), "why, Abe can go through a rick like grain through a goose." They all piped up with their two cents' worth, "Why there ain't nobody can fell buckeyes and hickories like Abe. Why he can carry the load of three men and two horses. We wuz movin' our chicken coop, weighed nigh on six hundred pounds and that boy picks it up just like a baby, carried it over and puts her down fine as silk. For four-corner bull pen I like him on my side. And he can read besides—a book inside his shirt and a burr under his tail and he's a roarin' wind on a stud horse."

"Why he ain't so tall," said Allen Gentry, who was tall enough but skinny. "Measure up, measure up," they all cried. Allen had build-ups on his shoes and he stretched his spine as high as it would go along the wall and Dennis Hanks, Abe's cousin, made a mark and Abe began to unravel and Allen said, "Well I thought I was tall."

"Well," said Abe, straightening himself still higher, "there's more to come and a good deal more. I have a good deal of come-out in me." And he came out two inches higher, to the laughter of the company.

"I seen him pick up a forty-four gallon barrel," Gentry said. "He's just the man to take my produce downriver before the ice comes." He and Abe looked at each other, taking a measure that would show who would keep a deal, pay honest, fight hard.

"Wall," another said, "Abe's full o' fun but I never see him dance or court a gal, and he can't sing no more'n a crow. So he wouldn't be stopping in at the taverns below the cliffs, that's for sure and sartin."

"How you come out on your case?" Crawford asked him, and Breckenridge started to tell about how Abe tried his first case. This John Dill and his brother, Lin, put up some protest about Abe running his raft out to the middle of the Ohio and ferrying people to both shores. So they jumped him one day and said they aimed to duck him to learn him something. Abe said, "I'm the strongest buck around this lick," and he mussed them up. "What you gonna learn me?" he said.

"Yore takin' money out'n our pockets," they said, so they brought him to court for beating on them too.

So Abe had to go one morning in the spring across the river to Squire Pete's, who held court in his house, and Abe was his own lawyer and held trial and said to himself, "Cricky, it's good to have words on your tongue. I'm a lawyer now for sure." The Squire shook his hands and said, "Come over any time to court." So he did that. David Turnham, the constable in Gentryville, talked law talk to him and gave him a book about Indiana where he read, "We hold these truths to be self-evident, that all men are created equal"—and he had pondered this in his heart.

Dennis Hanks broke himself off a chaw of 'baccy. "It ain't in the nature of a man to be larnin' from books all the time. He can read streams, trees, the weather—larnin' from sich is the province of a man, but books—"

"He is a smart boy," Mr. Breckenridge said, and put his lace cuffed hand on Abe's shoulder. "Reading maketh a full man." And Abe already looked down at the handsome head, with the crow's-wings hair thickly crowning his brow, and saw his claw-hammer coat with brass buttons, his fancy waistcoat and bug-tight trousers, and the frilled bosom of his shirt, the lace of which he fingered with his white hands. Abe read his meaning clear—leave the riffraff of your people; leave the crowded cabin and the hunger and the driving need to keep moving and

moving; leave the lonely graves of the early dead
from toil and privation; leave the axe and the awl
and the labor and the common knowing. The gen-
tleman's clothes and the laughter and storytelling
and the fine words drew him like a poultice to steal
across the river or climb the bluffs to the brick
courthouse and listen to the well-dressed, the
ruffled, the sweet-scented and the golden-tongued,
the Philadelphia lawyers, as his pa called them. How
they could cheat and wrangle and slip a man right
out of his own skin! And after the court the judge,
the jury, the witnesses in the gentlemen's parlor,
with the courtyard and windows filled with people,
hoping to hear the golden words and the tall tales
and the funny stories; the jokes would pass out the
window and be told down the street and the people
would stamp their feet, and cry hurrah, and hold
their sides from laughing.

Mr. Breckenridge was a proslavery man, and you
had to protect yourself from the cunning of his words
as from a poisonous berry. But McSweeney edged up
and thrust himself between Abe and Mr. Breckenridge, shaking his fist and his huge red head so his
starved body shook. When he was excited his glasses,
tied around his ears, fell off, and his long horse lip

quivered and he shook in his faded coat that covered the scars of the Irish revolution where his brothers had been hanged for liberty's sake. He shook his long finger. "Here are all your bosses, Abe Lincoln, set in judgment on ye, scrounging out yore blood. Suckers, eels they are. Crawford—what does he pay you fer looking after his store, running his ferry?"

"I pay him a good sum," Blue Nose said, "for a man who is behind every haycock with his nose in a book."

"Ah ha," McSweeney cried, "two bits a day sunup to sundown, and makin' him work shuckin' corn three days to pay for a lousy book by Parson Weems that got spoiled in the rain."

"It was shore wuth it," Abe said, letting himself down and hitching his long legs one over the other. "All about Valley Forge and George Washington."

"He ain't no hand to pitch into his work like killin' snakes," Old Blue Nose said. "'You know how to kill hogs?' I asked him. 'If you risk yore hogs,' sez he, 'I'll risk Abe Lincoln.'"

"It's cinchy pay," McSweeney said. "And runnin' the raft out to pick up them mid-river passengers from them new steam buggies. . . ."

"It's wuth it fer nuthin'," Abe said, and he put his feet onto the fire hearth and realized how the fall

cold of death had gone into his bones, and it was good to be with this joshing and cruel joking, attacks and counterattacks, knowing always what stood, like a huge shadow, falling over the tiny jibe of their speech and their show of courage. "The Ohio River," Abe said, "has become a big highway fer everybody to go down—fur traders, slave catchers, gamblers, farmers, rich men, poor men, moguls, and thieves, and every kind of boat you can set yore mind on—broadhorns, flatboats loaded with pork, grain whiskey, ginseng—why I even saw a church smack dab in the middle of the raft and the preacher prayin' all git-out to the catfish!" Abe felt the men settling to a story and he crossed one long branch of his leg over the other one and began to waggle it up and down in tune to his thoughts. "Well sir, today I picked up two gentlemen. I took my raft out, took their trunks onto it and one of them said, 'I never thought to see a scarecrow in the middle of the Ohio River.'" The men on the cracker barrels all howled and hawed. "And after I'd taken their trunks to shore these gentlemen of the east threw a silver dollar on my flatboat—a silver dollar. There it lay—I never saw one before. For this little labor I'd earned in one hour a silver dollar— there it was, big as life—"

"Well, ye see he's growin' too big fer his britch-es," they said. "He'll be goin' east to put his dollar in Biddle's bank. He'll be ownin' some slaves o' his own. Our Abe'll be settin' in with the southern gentry. Tell the story," they said, "of the lizard got in the preacher's pants . . . ."

Forgotten now was the night, the graves on the hill, the howling of the panthers, the darkness falling east from the westering sun—forgotten the tomorrows of heavy toil. Abe licked and mouthed a story, wrung it out, hung it out to dry, shook it loose, raveled it, unraveled it, and shook it out in all its laughter and meaning. Everyone settled down with looks of anticipation and pleasure. You always got into Abe's stories, carefully flung out like a lasso. He made a dazzling package, wrapped, then flung it open, and the meaning continued to skyrocket and burst in you the next day as you stopped at the mill, in the furrow, at the planting, the reaping and the grinding—to let out a big haw-haw, savoring the jokes and stories of this lanky boy who pinned you, at the same time as he told you jokes, with the saddest eye ever hung within the high, tall dome of man born of woman.

They all settled down to their stout and 'baccy as Abe said, "Well sir, there we wuz, listenin' to that walkin' preacher, who could whip everyone up to singin', shoutin', speakin' in tongues—a bean pole of a man, lanker'n me, from Kaintuck, rusty coat tail, stiff collar—he made a picture with his frontier dignity showin' and an Adam's apple pumpin' up and down like a bucket, droppin' into a well and pulling up the words out of the slimy deeps. The only danger I saw it might have swallowed up his little head, unraveled it entirely. Well, everyone was snorin' after the third hour and he was shoutin' on his text which was—'God hath chosen the foolish things of the world to confound the wise'—when a little foolish thing, a lizard, streaked up his pants. I guess brought on by the warmth of the snoring people, the lizard thought it was summer. It darted up the preacher's sleeve and slid down his collar and the preacher leaped higher and shouted louder and ripped off his collar. The lizard then descended into Hell where the preacher was aflinging the disbelievers and he ripped off his coat and the lizard leaped up on his shoulder blades and by this time we was all scratching away and the preacher was flinging his arms behind himself, tying them in a knot, turning his head clean around, ripping off his shirt. His hair stood up, the audience woke up, startled, and then old Mrs. Grigsby says in a prim voice, 'You might as well give up, Reverend, he's sure to get into your pants,' and the whole congregation rocked and roared . . . ." And so did the listeners around the fire that late fall night. "And it's the first time I ever had a good time in church, and I suppose it's sinful."

It was not long, whenever men came together, before the talk got around to politics, and soon there was spirited talk about Old Hickory Jackson running for President, about the Indian wars, and slavery, with Mr. Breckenridge saying that the North was only green with envy that they did not have cheap labor like the slaves. "Don't look at me," Abe says. "I'm an indentured slave to my pa till I'm twenty-one and my pa always said in Kaintuck, and it was one of the reasons he come on to Indianny, that a white man could not make a living while there were black slaves."

"Nonsense," said Mr. Breckenridge, in his best court manner. "Negroes are like children, they need slavery."

Abe felt his heart pound to answer so boldly such a famous man as Mr. Breckenridge but he had to say it, "I've heard it all my life that it is good to be a slave. The British tried to make my grandfathers like it. As the boy said skinning an eel—'It don't hurt 'em so much, not so very much. They're used to it!' Well, if you're the eel you might feel mighty different! Besides, I never heard of the man who wishes to take the good of slavery by being one hisself, have you, Mr. Breckenridge?"

"You have to have slaves," Mr. Breckenridge said, "to found a great civilization, a flowering culture." And the schoolteacher, Mr. McSweeney, rose up and his red wig fell askew, and he said he wouldn't flower in the stink of slavery, and upon the bodies of black brothers. He spoke of the shame of black slavery only a few years after they had fought to make men free; and New England now with one hundred and fifty ships hauling these shameful oversea cargoes of human beings, packed spoon fashion between decks like sardines, ironed together, flogged and starved; and what was a Christian man doing in such traffic even if he could double his money in six months, dealing in human flesh. And he cried out that there would be a bloody war, that all the rivers would run red with blood and brother would fight brother in America yet.

Abe had to stand by McSweeney for the scars of battle upon his flesh and he wanted to stand by the ill-starred men who fought and sometimes lost, who had, like his fathers and mothers, lights and torches that sprang alive and lighted the brains and hearts of men in the darkness of time.

"Well, I don't know the right of slavery," Abe said, "but I think the proslavery arguments are thin as soup made by boiling the shadow of a pigeon that has starved to death! I know this much clear and simple—I wouldn't want to be a slave."

"That's right, Abe, we fought and died, faced the storm, and should we pay the wolf? We began by declaring all men are created equal and now we say all except Negroes, and when the slavery know-nothings get control we'll read the Constitution to say all except Negroes, foreigners, and Catholics."

"The church's agin' it," the men said, seriously, chewing the cud of an awful problem. There was talk of a man in Illinois, who had freed all his slaves and given them a parcel of land. One thing was sure—they would chase slaveowners out of the new state of Indiana where every man had a chance to get on in the world.

"Abe, what you gonna be when you grow up?" Dennis asked.

That was a good one—"Grow up," they all cried. "How high you gonna be, Abe?"

"Well," Abe said, "my legs touch the ground and that's all that's needed. I guess I'll have to be President of the United States, if a tough one like Old Hickory—"

"President!" they all howled. "Seven-foot Abe Scarecrow in the White House. Mr. President," they howled. Abe swung his legs, grinning, running his grubby fingers through his stiff black hair.

Breckenridge rose to go, and shook Abe's hand, and asked him to come to court whenever he wanted; and they heard the sound of his big bay team, the finest in the country; and Abe turned back to the men he loved, the ignorant, plain men who had their hands on the wooden handles of axe, and plow, and wheel, plain men like himself in butternut jeans.

"I don't know the right of slavery," Abe said. "It's somethin' I'll have to dig out like a stump, run it to the fiber, dig it out, and hold it up plain so I kin see its kind and habits and make it plain to all minds like my own."

"You think too much," Mr. Gentry, the biggest landowner in the parts, said. "You could amount to somethin', Abe, if you'd keep yore nose out'n them books."

"Mr. Gentry," Abe said. "There's some argumentation about what use a man is that lends money out at big interest that breaks the back of the settler."

"Yore pa is a no-good huntin' man, don't tend to his acres."

"My pa works longer, harder, digs deeper, plants oftener than any man in these parts, and the interest goes to you."

"No need to get huffy. I got a proposition to make to you, Abe. I got a load of pork, flour, and sundry I'd like to see what it would bring in New Orleans. Now I hear you got a raft. How'd you like to go with my son Allen here, under his command of course, down the river?"

"Allen ain't no river man."

"Air you, Abe Lincoln? I been as far down as you."

"That's just about round the bend as fur as your eye can see."

"You'd work the stern sweep, Abe." Abe grinned, seeing this tall thin boy holding the big scow in the channel of the orneriest, meanest, curlingest, most uncertain, wandering, tail-twisting river, that old Mississippi. But his brain caught fire, snagged on the words and burned—down the big river, down the heart of the continent with the big men, the Mike Finks, the river roarers. He saw himself breasting her down; easing her round the bends, down the sugar coasts past Memphis, Natchez, Vicksburg, down into the summer; tying up at strange settlements; hearing the talk of traders, pirates, gamblers, gypsies around campfires where you fried catfish big as a man. He would test his skill against the sleds, barges, pirogues, dugouts, sailing skiffs, and now the big lighted steamboats hooting, blowing black smoke, and lighted at night with black men firing the boilers, and, above, dancing on the decks, men and women in curled wigs, lace, and velvet.

"You'd trust me, Mr. Gentry, to take your goods down?"

"Don't know anyone, Abe, I'd trust more and my son Allen too, my only son."

"Will you hold my pa's debt till I get back?"

"Sure will that."

"How much you pay?"

"Eight a month and grub."

"And my way back?"

"Well, it would be mighty good experience for you to work yore way back on one of those newfangled steamers."

"Hold out," McSweeney said. "Make the old skinflint pay yore passage back."

"My way back," Abe said.

"To St. Louis?" Gentry said.

"To St. Louis if Allen has to hike it from there with me. Be good experience for him. Learn to rough it."

"I'll give you that farm when you get back, Allen," Gentry said. "Abe'll make a man of you."

"Oh I don't know," Abe said. "Wouldn't want to interfere with the Almighty's intentions." The men all howled. "We'll take off soon's we load her. The cold days are comin' on mighty swift."

"Signs," Dennis said, "are fer a cold winter. Who's gonna cut wood for the fire?"

"You," Abe said, bundling Dennis up and pushing him out the door amidst the laughter of the men, for it was well known Dennis was the best liar and the worst woodcutter in Pigeon Creek.

Abe felt light and dizzy as he and Dennis hit the dark for home.

CHAPTER 5

DENNIS AND ABE started up the ridge for home but Abe turned down toward Anderson's creek for he wanted to see his raft now. Dennis full of stout had to trot to keep up with Abe's easy long-legged swing.

"You don't touch a drop but you're drunk on words, Abe," Dennis mumbled to himself. "I'm only old Dennis Hanks, who'll never see over the horizons you will. I'm not much older'n you, Abe. It was me ran down the pike that day, February 12, when yore ma borned you in a little log cabin in Kaintuck, the dark and bloody ground, and I said this is a yaller swamp baby and he won't amount to much. And now look at ye, goin' down the river with yore own raft and eight dollars a month. Whoopee!" Dennis was like those new steamboats. When they blew their whistle they stopped in midstream—when he hollered he toppled over. Abe picked him up, stood him on his pins and trotted on with Dennis following and, as always, when Dennis was with Abe he had thoughts that didn't grow on his own bough. The way he had it figgered, these thoughts shook off Abe's high bough onto him, like ripe, tart apples, and he could gather some of them. He didn't naturally have the long thoughts, the ideas from books, because he couldn't read and had no hankering for it, but he had grown up with Abe, fished him out of creeks, plucked him from the panther's path; and all his life—and he lived long after Abe was gone—he told of every little thing that happened. He thought he was like a coyote that travels under the belly of a buffalo, warms himself, eats his leavings, and gets the security of traveling with the best fighter, forager, the strongest and the quickest.

And now the tears fell on his face as he remembered Abe was leaving, and his mind was stewing like poor man's soup, where you put in everything; and then he heard Abe singing in a high, squeaky voice:

The turbaned Turk
That shuns the world
And struts about
With his whiskers curled
For nobody else
But himself to see.

Dennis began to sing—"With his whiskers curled—with his whiskers curled," but he could not sing and trot and puff after those long legs, and he thought of all the times they had sung at Sinking Springs in the woods of Kentucky; of all the trees they had cut together, the locusts, the gum, ash, and poplars, the red bush, the dogwood; all the cradles they had cut the wood for, beds and coffins, gun handles, roofs, doors and the hearths; how they together had chopped, planed, carved, split, cut, pegged, and sawed it all. Nobody knows the grain, strength, weakness, nature, willingness, and stubbornness of a piece of wood like you, Abraham. Putting your hands on the wood, planning which way for its fall, which wood likes to bear a dead weight like hickory, and how the willow likes to bend easy, and the nature and willingness of the sassafras, pawpaw, gum, burr, oak, elm, sugar maple, pine, beech, and oh, the groves of white oak we laid our axe to, Abe my friend, my cousin, brother axeman, wilderness orphan like me.

Now Dennis Hanks had many of the thoughts he was later to have when Abe was President, and he wore a stovepipe hat like him, and tried to walk and talk like his cousin Abe, and told many truths and many lies at the White House, but it was true, as he said, when he went there to see Abe, he "gathered me into his arms." Dennis told about it, bragging a little, after Abe was long dead. "I taught Abe his first lesson in spelling, with a buzzard's quill," he bragged. This was funny as he had to make excuses that he could not write, saying "his ink was froze," then, bragging some more, "Nobody else does not know so much about Abe. It depends upon me to tell about it. In Indianny then thar was bear, deer, turkeys, and coon, wildcats and other things and frogs. We had meetings and sang, *Oh When Shall I See Jesus?* and *Rain with Him Above.* And one of Abe's favorites was a song about the Turpenturk that scorns the world and struts about with his whiskers curled. Abe never could sing much." So he wrote it out painfully years later when Abe was gone. Told about such a night as this one, "He was so odd, original, humorous, and witty that all the people in town would gather around him. He would keep them there till midnight or longer telling stories and cracking jokes. I would get tired, want to go home; cuss Abe most heartily."

In this far year of 1828, Dennis could hear the tall boy, Abe, singing, croaking out the song in the frosty, fall night.

By hokey day, Dennis thought, trotting along behind a long-legged, ragged, worried, melancholy scarecrow of a boy growing every which way, exploding like a pumpkin vine in wet weather. That Abe grows out of the dark like me, but he reaches further. He worries a thought till it bursts apart for him, thrusts his head up, sees over horizons. Don't let him go down that awful river, Lord, humble child of the backwoods like me. I'm jest a pore white, a lean and hongry backwoodsman. The in and out of pressing nature against Abe turns him into something different than me. Born of sisters, in the same weather, the same land, the same days, growing out of the low, dark, common life, slowly, strongly, Abe grows to the stars. I grow slow and close to the ground, but I can look at him from down here below in the brush, by hokey.

Trotting after Abe, he remembered how he had come up with his Aunt and Uncle Sparrow to Indianny, how they had all lived in the threefaced camp, that first spring at Pigeon Creek and the last spring of that delicate girl, Nancy Hanks; how they had eaten wild turkey, and that heathen, Nancy, had sung and danced; and Abe had shot a turkey gobbler, and then said he would never shoot a living thing again; how Abe gave the boys a lecture when they were burning a fire on the back of a turtle, how he had written a regular sermon about cruelty. By hokey, he had picked that turtle up and you would have thought it was his buried brother.

I seen you cryin', Abe, in the wilderness, sprung from nothin'—Abe, an untried green sapling but already getting a strong heartwood. Who's gonna speak to us, Abe, on the violent waters? Who's gonna bear our sorrows and turn our terror into stories of laughter? He's a star from Pigeon Creek, and if he should die the little children would cry in the wilderness.

Then there was that time after Nancy Hanks lay asleep under the feet of deer, and Abe had got him a paper tore out of a speller, and with a buzzard quill and poke berries for ink, he had spelled out a note to

David Elkin, the sky pilot, to come in the spring to say a sermon for Nancy who put much store by such things. And those worm twistings on the paper really spoke to the preacher, and shore enough he come in the spring, and the neighbors gathered on the ridge, and he spoke good words that fell down like honey to that girl, Nancy Hanks, below the sod.

By hokey, Dennis thought, ef'n he goes I'll have to be cutting the wood and I ain't got the heft, ain't nobody can blaze and cut a tree and put a chain around her and drag her to the fire like Abe. I'm too short fer it, and Tom ain't no farmer for that rocky, weedy, scrubby, knotty, knobby land. We'll be pore as poverty.

Then he had a terrible thought. Suppose Abe was destined, like Moses, who turned the sea and led his people through. Maybe he was walkin' behind a man full o' destiny. Why Abe even told him that the sun does not move. He's a prophet. Why that's only old Abe up front there, we've plowed it, grubbed it, mowed and cradled, gathered, winnowed, shucked, and reaped . . . . "Abe . . . Abe," he yelled.

"Hey, hey," Abe kept calling out of the darkness and shouting back, "Oh the terrible Turk that scorns the world and struts about with his whiskers curled."

They squatted on the ridge for a breath. "You got to learn readin' and cipherin', Dennis. Now there's a piece Miss Hodgens has about Robinson Crusoe—you'd like that. Now there's things in books I got to know."

"What kind o' things, Abe?"

"All kinds of things. I don't even know what's in those books to know what kind of things to look for in those books. I got to think on it quiet like, not in a cabin full o' wormy kids, and my old man with the shakes, and his land bein' taken out from under him. I got to figure why some say, 'You toil and earn bread and I'll eat it.' We got this here now not from the mouth of a king but the same tyrannical principle, an excuse for one race enslaving another race. I got to think out what's the common right of humanity and what's the right of kings."

"It's a mighty chawfull. Ain't you skeered, Abe?"

"Shore I'm skeered."

"You gonna carry a gun? Suppose you git killt?"

"I ain't got a gun. If I git killed, I can't die but oncet." They heard the boats hooting on the Ohio just down the hill. They could see the raft riding the slight swell of Anderson's Creek—a long, heavy, flat-bottomed scow that would float down to New

Orleans with the current but never come back. It would be steered by long oars at either end and would slide over snags and shallows where a keel boat could never go.

"Look," Dennis shouted. "Pirates." Dark figures were scurrying on the raft. Abe gave a whoop and started sliding down the bluff, yelling, "Come on, men, whet yore horns, get at 'em," as if he had a whole regiment with him. He caught one and held young Grigsby, known as Whining Billy, a sniffler, whiner, and tattler. He held him up by the scruff of the neck then smacked him on the bottom and squealing, the kid ran into the dark. They saw that the bow oar had been smashed. "I'll take the sweep off the Grigsby raft," Abe said.

"I'm a river man," Dennis said. "Let me go with you, Abe."

"A river man you are not," Abe laughed. "Neither am I. We're tree men, Dennis. You stay with yore wife and baby, and Sarah Bush'll be in need of wood and water."

"How we gonna get by without you, Abe?" They squatted on the raft which rose and fell gently with the backwash from the Ohio and they looked down into the darkness where the river went a thousand miles through the heart of America. "Don't worry, Dennis," Abe said. "We'll make it."

"You got a feeling, Abe, yer equal to anything. That's the new democratic man free of any man above him, tips his hat to nobody."

Abe laughed, "I'm superior if not equal. That's the democratic man."

"You ain't got no sense of a man stayin' where he is."

"Why, where should a man stay? We'd of stayed in the old country with kings and lords. Man can do what he wants; the stars are the limit. He can raise the whole tide of man. All he got to do is rise out of superstition; learn to see clear without fear or favor."

"I can see you, Abe, shining, rising from the lowest swamp like marsh lights, like gas set on fire by its own get-up, rising, blazing out clear and bright." That's the way it was. You were always seeing a new Abe—like finding a tree suddenly in the forest when the autumn cleaned the leaves, or you cut down one, and there suddenly you could see a new tree, or over a hill into the distance.

"We'll miss ye, Abe."

"Dennis, I'll miss you, but I'll take ye all with me and be with you always . . . for to this place"—and he thought of the blue flowers on the grave of

Nancy Hanks and her waiting there—"and these people"—and he thought of all their patience, strength, suffering, silence, slow speech that lived in him, for which he was sign and signal. "To this place and these people and this"—he thought of the ideas of freedom so warm and near in all he knew, fifty years from the days they shed their blood for land, and equality and brotherhood.

"Wicked men might kill you, Abe." Dennis turned his face into the darkness to hide his tears.

"If they do kill me I shall never die again. I got a kind of poem I wrote. Want to hear it, Dennis?" Faltering, sad he read it, some of the lines his own, some he had read and made his own:

> *Time what an empty vapor 'tis*
> *And days, how swift they are*
> *Swift as an Indian arrow*
> *Fly on like a shooting star.*
> *The present moment just, is here*
> *Then slides away in haste,*
> *That we can never say they're ours*
> *But only say they're past.*

"Oh," Dennis howled. "That's mighty sad, Abe Lincoln. Go it, go it on the tide to glory, Abe Lincoln."

Abe caught him by his buckskin jacket or he would have fallen into the stream. "I'll go it, Dennis," Abe said, "and you go it here. Stand up for yore belief even if yore alone. I'll stand up for mine and we'll see this through."

On the way back all the lights had gone out in the cabins, and Abe strode on ahead of Dennis toward their home place through the dark brush in a gaunt and lonely melancholy.

CHAPTER 6

SARAH BUSH LINCOLN was listening for Abe. The fall night was late and the tiny cabin was full of sleeping children and Tom Lincoln groaning and worrying in his sleep. She was a strong, dark woman, moving among the pallets on the floor where nine children slept. Dennis Hanks' wife, one of Sarah's daughters, and his new baby slept in the three-legged bed on a bear rug. Sarah was fixing the rising bread for morning baking.

She feared Abe had gone even now, down the river. He was set on leaving and what would she do when the wolves howled outside the fire glow and the trees cracked with cold? But oh, she thought, if he goes away now; if he leaves and the big snows come—and Dennis Hanks not one to haul the big fallen trees out of the snow with log chain and axe to make them for the hearth fire.

Who will bring in some hog fat from the butcher-ing, or a sack of corn for grinding? "Oh, Abe Lin-coln," she cried, kneading the bread. What was it in this strange, tall boy who had moved into her heart as no one ever had? He was her loneliness, he was her refuge in time of trouble, as the Bible said, the chopper of wood, and the carrier of water.

Since the first time, in the spring, when she had come up the Pigeon and seen Abe and his sister, Sarah, gaunt, lonely, half-starved, and afraid, she had loved them as her own. When Tom Lincoln, wife-less, had come back to Elizabethtown to find a wife, she had accepted him and, with her three fatherless children, her handmade rugs, her hickory-withe fur-niture, she had crossed the river and taken to her heart the two lorn children of Nancy Hanks; cut them out of their smelling buckskins; washed them; clothed them in her own linsey-woolsey; fed and warmed them; and made Abe a loft where he could burn a candle at night and read his precious books.

Now she thought he was at the grave of his dead mother. Sarah could never get him to call her Ma. She never knew a young'un to beat—a bit teched, some said—all that study from the books, and his gloomy nature—and a man he was, and it wasn't right to keep him tethered. She would get away from that crowded cabin if she could. He's growed too fast, she told herself, six-foot-four, sticking out of his pants like a colt; but he could lick his weight in wildcats just the same.

Tom Lincoln riz up from his pallet on the floor and looked at her with his one eye. "What you doin', Sary?"

"You know what I'm adoin'," Sarah whispered. "Lay back and rest and stop thinkin' what you owe that shark Gentry."

He lay back. "I cain't help thinkin'. Maybe I should take that other mortgage. I could maybe clear another acre, plant more, maybe have something like Gentry to take down the river to sell or trade."

Sarah kneaded the good dough. "Don't think about it now, get yore rest."

"What ef'n Abe plans to run off and leave me?"

"He's agrowin' up and needs more larnin' than he can find hereabouts."

Tom rankled. "Larnin'. All that stuff. Why look at me. I make a mark on the rafters when somebody owes me and then rub it out when they pay."

"Yes, look at you," Sarah laughed. But she was thinking how even in Kentucky Nancy Hanks saw to it Abe was around learning. She brought Dr. Graham of Knob Creek to the cabin and picked his brains for Abe. Christopher Columbus Graham, a doctor scientist, studying minerals and plants, came and told Abe a mighty raft of things. And that Audubon used to walk around painting birds in Elizabethtown. Every lawyer, traveler, teacher, politician, and peddler Nancy brought in, to plant her son Abe with any acorn of knowledge they might have in their tall brains.

"What in tarnation is that on your whitewashed ceiling, Sary?" Tom asked.

"It's Abe's footprints!" Sarah's shoulders shook. "Ain't he the caution!" She had whitewashed the whole inside of the cabin to get away from the infernal darkness, the root silence, with the only light coming through the one small window; and Abe had put shoes on his hands, and made tracks, of all places, on the ceiling. She had laughed so heartily that he had laughed with her—for the first time—and had even read her what he wrote in his spelling book with a neat scratching, like a dove's tracks on snow: "Abraham Lincoln, his hand and pen. He will

be good, but God knows when." A caution for wildcats that Abe! And Oh Lordy, she had stopped up
the cracks in the logs with his Louisville paper. He
would raise all Hades! Tom was mumbling, "A
man's got a right to his son till he's twenty-one—a
man's got some rights."

When he was asleep, Sarah was left alone with her
thoughts of Nancy Hanks, that gay girl she had
known in Kentucky, that dancer and singer, that
laugher, that runner in the woods, and now she often
spoke softly to the sweet ghost of Nancy Hanks—"I
give yore daughter Sarah the best wedding, all the
fixings—fat wild turkeys, saddles of deer, vegetable
pies, wild honey and ripened pawpaws, and coffee
and cream for Mrs. Grigsby, the groom's ma. But
you know they work a woman in the wilderness
worse'n a hoss, and she died when her child was born
without a granny woman, and I didn't have time to
git thar. Who but you knows the life of a wilderness
woman—the winters, the planting, the harvesting,
the lean years to fill the pot with a bony squirrel or a
jaybird, and all the day of toil and haying in the low
meadows by the light of the moon. Lord," she cried,
"You are my shepherd, I shall not want. Look down
on this humble child of the backwoods, on the son of

Nancy Hanks and Sarah Bush—two lowly hand-maidens. He's agoin' down that great and dangerous river, I know it; protect him as You protect the meek and lowly. Forgive me that my brother in Kentuck is a slave-catcher, buying mothers and children like sheep. Let Abe be a man with the love of right, draw reasons and lessons from Your beasts and weeds and the lowly Women in the flax. Let him stand for his beliefs like You in the face of Herod and his persecutors, and let him always stand for Nancy Hanks and Sarah Bush who are only women and have no voice and no rights. Let Abe stand for us in the councils of the mighty, in the market place, in the temples of the Philistines . . . ."

With the quick ear of a woman often alone in the wilderness, she heard Abe approach the cabin. She wiped her floury hands, quickly and silently opened the door, and stepped out into the pitch, cool, fall night lifting her apron around her shoulders. "Abe—Abe—" she called into the darkness.

He answered, and she went toward him. "Yes ma'm."

"Kin I talk to you, Abe?" She felt for him in the dark.

"Yes ma'm." She felt his sadness even in the dark. "I smell 'baccy smoke. You been to the tavern. I smell night woods too. You been wrastlin' with yore angel, Abe?"

"Well," he drawled above her, and she felt the protection and tenderness of his presence. "There ain't room in that cabin to wrastle even with yore angel who might be tall as a thimble. And you put my *Louisville Journal* for stuffing in the cracks. Clay's speech in thar."

"I took'n hit out Abe. I cain't please you, Abe. I guess it's cause I give you a bath first time I seen you."

She felt he was grinning, but his sadness came down upon her like autumn smoke. "Cut us out'n our buckskin we had on fer months; larded our heads fer nits; scrubbed us with lye soap; took'n the pole-cat smell off'n us; threw the bed shucks to the hogs; and stirred us up corn bread and middlin'. I shore hold it agin you, ma'm. Only one thing I got agin you, ma'm, yore fam'ly is slave-catchers. I don't hold to that."

"I don't hold to hit neither, Abe." She could hear Dennis singing in the thicket.

"You don't? I got to tell you and you tell my pa—I got a job tonight with Gentry, takin' his stuff down the river. Day after tomorrow—but I'll stack up a month's fire fer you, ma'm."

Her heart went cold but now she knew she was glad and wished she was a young man footloose and free. "You comin' back in the spring, time fer plantin'?" She knew he didn't intend to come back but waited for him to tell her as she knew he would.

"I don't aim to come back. Beggin' yore pardon, ma'am, I aint gonna stay in my father's cabin. Sarah gone, ain't nothin' fer me. I got to find out—what's down there, what's happenin'."

"Abe, you got yore people to think on, and it ain't jest yore pa's family. We didn't break away from King George to take up the slave trade and fatten on our brother, did we?"

"Why, I didn't know you had those idees."

"You never asked me," she said. "Nobody ever asked me." Go—go, she said in her heart, go down the river to understanding, mix with the people, the country. If I was a young man I'd go this night, without all those mouths to feed.

He took her calloused, cracked, dirt and doughed hand. "I'll send you somethin' to put in the childern's mouths."

She let her hand go in his big calloused hand as he held it tightly. "They ain't yore kith or kin. You find what yore hankerin' fer. I'll fix it with yore pa. He'd go, too, like a shot if'n he could. A swamp of mosquitoes is buzzing in his ears. It's his debts. He'll bide down."

"Gentry ain't goin' to press him. I'll send somethin' back."

"The Almighty look down on you, son," she said. "And do His work in the world—too many worship Mammon. With the taxes goin' sky high we're gettin' not only black slaves but white slaves. We got to uphold what we always been fightin' fer and always will."

"I didn't know you was of those opinions—Ma," he said, and put his big hand on her head.

She felt like a girl as he embraced her shoulders, and she leaned against him for a moment and she was at home now, at ease, for she had a talker and a fighter in her house—and in the house of America.

"Come in and sleep, Abe," she said, taking his big hand, and he followed her.

"I'll sleep, Ma," he said.

CHAPTER 7

THE NEXT DAY Abe put the Grigsby raft oar on his raft. His pa got up early and went hunting so Abe knew that Sarah had told him he was going away. They were ready to load her, and Abe was proud of his raft. He had cut every log himself, notching only the straightest, the strongest, poplar butts and oak. He had blazed them in the spring and summer mornings, before and after work, with axe, draw knife, and saw, he had pegged and cleated and cut out wooden pins to mortise the corners solid. The uprights were six feet, the bottom was double to store the goods within, the chest, post and setting pole, the two long oars at bow and stern were from the best hickory. In the middle was a small, roofed cabin for fires and sleeping in rainy weather.

Now the raft was the strength of his own body, and with it he would test his skill against the river. He would leave the forests, the plains, the prairies, and the hills. He had been a tree man all his life, chopping his way west on land with others of his kind. He had flung his tiny strength since a stripling himself into the great sunless forests of Kentucky, against the poplar and oak of Indianny; the swing of the axe made the way he walked, the way he talked, the rhythm of his heart and sinew; the tree had been a book which he had opened, and read, and learned of men and strength, of time and its markings.

He had smoothed, whittled, soaked, and mauled with a new axe handle of hickory, that fitted his hand and swung like a stiff whip. It was much better than the old axes brought from Europe which were light and brittle in the helve and did not swing with the body of the new man, meeting a new wilderness.

He could take the measure of a tree very well by his eye, and it helped him later to take the measure of a man. There was white oak, hickory, walnut, and buckeye, white oak for splitting for rails or the moldboard of the plow; there was hickory for new helves, and ramrods, for guns and withes. Everything was harder to do with hickory but always better done. It had the greatest heat and smoky smell, and made strong wheels, had a sinew, grain you couldn't split, slow to growth and late to flower, sweet in fruit and strong in maturity, ice couldn't split it or summer heat kill. It was tough, had a bend when you insisted.

Nancy taught him the shagbark dyes, yellow from oak, butternut hulls and sumac for red and yellow, rose red from poke berry and redroot; taught him to save the pearl elm ash for baking.

The hickory gave him back talk too. You had to plan the overthrow of a hickory. There you were in the wilderness needing rails and logs, coffins and cradles, and most of all heat against the cold and fire for the cooking. Abe felt like a demon vandal plotting the death of the ancient, bearded forest trees, planted, grown in time unknown to him. There he stood cunning, studying the tree's weakness, where to wedge in, which way to let it fall, how to strike against the centuries of strength, how to plan the wood's use, spoiling as little as possible, how to use the logic of the tree. There they stood—the green boy, the sapling man, and the ancient, bearded patriarch. At last you knew where to strike where the patriarch was sleeping and you took your seven-pound pardner, the axe you had made yourself, balanced in the hefting grip and you swung it back, letting it flow out from all your bone and sinew, breathing on the upswing and letting the air out on the blow; and the hickory, grown in time before Abe's birth, struck back, resisted the blow, sent back its resistance along the axe head, up the handle into your arms, shook the body down to the ground, rattled your teeth, as if the taut sinews of man, axe, and tree struck together. Sometimes, like a warrior, you had to change your strategy, wedge in another place, strike in again and again, all your strength into the down-clefting stroke, in rhythmic beat, again and again and again. The man's will in the wilderness struck through the just and accurate axe and the great old tree would have to give over, the holding and strength and knots binding together the memory of lost years would split, break to the deep-biting axe and man, and at last with a mighty crash, fall to the will of man, for door, and hearth and floor, cradle and coffin, bed and bludgeon, warmth and danger.

So Abe looked at his raft, gauging all its strengths along with his own and champing to be off as soon as possible.

The next day they had plenty of advice on loading the grain, flour, pork, and sundries into the hold. The banks were alive with people doing little work but talking plenty, saying they better get going, November was moving; the beavers were building high, fur was animal heavy; there would be an inch of ice in the holler in one day more; the freshes would be freezing in the Ohio.

Allen was dressed fit to kill—in black trousers tucked into polished eastern boots, and his black hair slicked down with goose grease. The remarks from the banks were hilarious. Allen Gentry must be goin' to catch more than catfish down there—what about them southern belles? They do hear tell it's mighty frolicsome in some of those places along the river. River talk moved up and down like pork and corn. They kept an eye on Abe who did most of the loading work. "Land o' Goshen," they said lovingly, "that boy sure is agrowin'." Juices and glands of that year's crop had made him grow, his wrists hung out of his buckskin coat, and his buckskin pants crawled up showing his bare white shanks, and his stiff black hair stuck out of his coonskin cap and his great, sad face was a dear thing to them all—although some mothers claimed it was a sight that made the babies cry. Forest living had made his face bark-rough like the trees he knew so well.

Allen had a trunk with his best clothes in it. All Abe had was tied up with a string—his linsey-woolsey suit Sarah made for him, prickly to the touch; some needles, threads, and buttons he would peddle if he could; and three books he had wrapped in a piece of buckskin against the weather—a Bible, the Parson Weems book on George Washington that cost him three days' work, and *Aesop's Fables*.

Big advice was shouted out while the men who had their harvest in now chawed and spit, gave advice, joked free and easy. "Tell 'em, Abe, we grow 'em tall up here and smart too. Don't let on Allen Gentry come from Indianny now. Git yoreself a fair plantation down thar. Not Abe, he don't aim to lord it over no man. Maybe you'll meet up with the salt river roarer hisself, the Ohio snapping turtle, Earthquake Billy, the ring-tailed squealer who, I heerd tell, can beat the daylights out o' you, Abe, for he clears an acre of land every time he swings his arms. Maybe you'll meet that villain, Jim Gerty, the swine. Maybe you'll meet Mike Fink, the half-horse, half-alligator man of the river."

But of all the guesses that day no one guessed that he would all but be killed on that journey, and it would change his whole life and help change the life of the nation.

But they didn't get started that day. Gentry had not killed all the hogs. November passed. Allen got a cold.

It was not till the morning of December 19, or thereabouts, that Allen and Abe were ready to shove off, and a goodly crowd of Gentryville men and women and children were there to see them start down the Ohio River.

Abe saw his pa and Sarah Bush, and when he told them good-bye and his pa didn't bawl him out but only said, "I'll niver set eyes on fur places like you, Abe," Abe knew Tom Lincoln was mourning his own youth and knew he would never be gallivanting off into the wide world again.

"Hurrah," Dennis Hanks yelled. "Hit her up to glory, Abe." And they all cried, "Whoopeeeee! Go it to glory, Abe Lincoln!"

Allen took his place at the stern sweep while Abe eased out the cable from the big cottonwood trunk, the raft took hold, swung out, and Abe heard his own voice queaking out, "Let 'er go!" Some wag yelled, "Stoke her, Gentry, yore bilers are frozen." The cable raced and Abe had to jump for the raft. He hauled in the cable, coiling it at the cabin, then he raced forward, got hold of the bow sweep, the shore moved away, and they were swept down the creek to the waving, shouting of the people of Little Pigeon Creek, wishing him well; he looked back on all he had known—the simple and honest men and women of toil, and he could hear their shouts for a long way, even after he saw the bluffs of Indiana and those of Ohio. They waved from the river bank and he felt he was being swept away from all he loved, as the bluffs of the grave of Nancy Hanks were swept away. He had to lean to the sweep as the current took them, and swept them past all native shores that they had known.

CHAPTER 8

ALLEN GENTRY gave orders from the stern like a captain, and Abe saw his white, scared face and the way he worked the oar frantically. Abe felt that the current would take you with its own reason, past snags, and hidden shelves or sand, but Allen was shouting, "Row—row," and Abe rowed.

In no time at all they shot by Evansville.

"Evansville," Allen shouted. Abe had been there many times but from the river it looked quite different. "Big Pigeon Creek," he shouted back, and before his voice moved out of his throat, they were past it, and he waved at some children whose shadows slanted back into the forest that rimmed the beach. It gave Abe a wonderful sense of time—of something passing you and yourself passing through.

75

Now he cried back to Allen, "Do you know the river beyond?"

Allen shouted back, "No, never been beyond."

So they faced the unknown river.

That night they tied up to a big cottonwood on the Kentucky side, and fell asleep as if they had been struck on the head by a crab apple billy. They woke early. Allen was stiff and sore and pale, but he still commanded the vessel.

As they pushed off into the current, Abe said, "I think we should stop rowing and follow the channel, let the raft take the current."

"I think we should use the oar," Allen said. "We'll use the oar and we'll get there quicker, and time is money."

"Time is certainly money to some," Abe said, and they pushed off.

"Remember, I'm taking this boat down," Allen said.

Abe obediently rowed. They passed all kinds of boats now, and some passed them and Abe learned to halloo back to them and pass jokes. But before noon they ran into a heavy fog. The air turned cold, and the water rose and hissed against the bow. Abe felt any moment they might hit a hidden floe or a planter, or sawyer, hidden logs that could rip the raft to pieces and put their cargo in the bottom of the river. He grasped the gouger ready to throw himself against it. He could not see the shore, and the fog was coming down far ahead of them.

"What can you see?" he shouted behind him.

"Nothing," came back through the fog, and he turned, and Allen was invisible and he could hardly see his own hand before his face.

"What can you see?" He heard Allen's voice.

"Nothing," Abe cried, and the fog filled his mouth.

"Keep a sharp lookout," Allen cried, as they veered around something that sharply struck the raft side, but it shook away. "To starboard," Allen shouted, before Abe could laugh at keeping your eyes open in that fog.

He shifted his weight, spread his legs wide, felt the boat respond to him except the rear, where he could feel the jerky rowing of Allen. "Let her go," he shouted. "Give her her head, let the current take her." But his words were lost in the thick cotton-like fog. The raft rocked and glided on, and all he could do was brace his long legs, grasp the sweep, peel back his eyes, and wait for anything. Once he saw the shore tilt by him; once he saw that they barely missed the stern wheel of an invisible steamboat.

Then suddenly, with Allen still yelling "Put to the oar," they seemed to be thrown out of the fog as if they had been in a tunnel, and rode suddenly into becalmed waters, then the current took hold of them again, swung the boat around, the bow lifted in the air, reared over a sand bar, gripped its mid-parts solid, and they were stranded.

The sweat stood on them, and Allen's face was white, and he was crying, "Lincoln, I told you to bend to it, to row. I told you. "

No water was getting into the cargo; they were fairly astraddle the bar, but Abe and Allen together could not lift it off. From the huddle of cabins three men rowed toward them—river men, logged, and sun-dried, tawny, lank men who didn't say much. "Well," one of them said, "you boys sure must've worked hard to git yoreself in this fix."

Allen said, "The river throwed us up here."

"River never throwed nobody on a sand bar; they most likely rowed themselves there. You boys rowin', wasn't you?"

Abe didn't say anything but Allen had the honesty to nod. "Well," they said, "don't never row. Let yourself go. Rowing throws you out'n the current.

You got a fur piece to go, let the river take you slow and easy, like a mother to you she'll be."

The men heaved them off easy as silk and, afloat again, Abe said, "Much obleeged to ye fer your advice."

"Better pull up here," the men said. "High jinks in the tavern there."

"Thanks," Abe said. "We'll pull down till dusk. We lost some time already." He gave a sly dig at Allen.

The light was golden and pale. Pretty soon Allen said, "Abe you were right. Maybe we better be kind of partners goin' down this river. I don't know much about rivers."

"Well," Abe said, heartily, "we can put our ignorance together, I reckon, and maybe we'll have a thimbleful of grit and gumption. This old river's got me beat for the now. Feel like I been wrastlin' everybody in Gentryville. She's a mighty muscular, mighty powerful old river—like a mother, he says—be with her and she'll cradle you down."

"I guess so, Abe. I'm glad yore my partner, Abe. I been a pretty big fool, but those men makin' cracks an' all . . . ."

"Never no mind, Allen Gentry. Let's head in now and sleep and grub and let that old mother rock us down."

CHAPTER 9

ALLEN SAID, "Do you think we will pass Cave-in-the-Rock by day or wait till the dark of the moon? I've heard it said the pirates wait day and night along the banks, and they'll be hungering for cargo like ours—flour and pork, for winter. They kill the rafters. Bones whiten along the river."

Abe looked back from the bow and saw the sharp white face of Allen and his fear, but he didn't fear river pirates or fog or wind. The water danced and rippled as they shot through the narrows and shoals, and he shouted back, "I'm more afeared of them rapids than any thieves. We'll be hittin' the Big Muddy where the catfish wear shovels on their noses to keep from chokin' to death. We're comin' to quiet water now, and I always notice it's quiet before the rapids." They flashed alongside a broadhorn, and Abe yelled, "Where you from?" and a bearded man funneled his hands and yelled back, "Massachusetts."

He watched boats of every description. Every bend brought them new sights. There were pirogues like giant canoes, swell-bodied galleys, barges widening in the middle, flatboats, arks, and broadhorns, so-called because of the pair of sweeps set clear forward like oxhorns. They passed big barges with a house in the middle, and crews at the sweeps, and kids and chickens and dogs and goats, and sometimes a rollicking fiddler in the evening, and dancing.

They were manned with oarsmen, slaves, peddlers; with farmers going to a new country with all their bag and baggage, kit and kaboodle. They were loaded with furs, flour, bacon, hides, leather, whiskey, sugar, tobacco, coffee going down; and they would bring back cotton, wines, and molasses and goods from foreign countries. There were barges with neat stores on them, fitted with shelves and counters of bolts, shoes, bonnets, hats, pans, and lanterns; there was a church and a gambling den, with men playing cards right in the sun.

The raft swept down the mighty river, past green-forested shores, rolling into prairies, cleared to set–

tlers. Abe sang, "We're bound through," and the torrents in himself were loosened to think of himself bound down the big river, a thousand miles through the beautiful Ohio, to the great Mississippi, a long spell of weeks to get there, and no return for him as for most in the wilderness.

Then, sure enough, the river began to quicken toward the falls. Abe peered into the moiling water, getting to know every sign of buried trees the river men called planters; and those called sawyers, that rode loosely on the current, were borne under, then bobbed up to trip you; and those called sleeping sawyers, hidden underneath. Then there were wooden islands just below the surface that could tear the bottom out of the raft, besides shoals, crosscurrents, sucking eddies, and the natural crookedness of the river, testing his skill and muscle and heft.

"Get set to yore sweeps, Allen," Abe yelled, as he felt an invisible hand reach out, lift the raft like a straw, spin her around so he had to lean his full weight, bring her slowly around, and point her down. The first thing he saw was a wrecked broadhorn laying up, tilted, her bow stuck into the water.

The raft began to twitch and buck under them, and they joined a mass of logs, rocks, branches, buckled endwise in the current, sweeping down over the falls. The channel was shallow, split by ripples and shoals, and Abe lay back to it, rode the thick butt of the sweep as the raft tilted to the rapids. He bent to the sweep and his eyes bugged out as he was lifted like straw, but he held on. His muscles swelled, his fingers hung on stiff, and he forced her into the swerve, held her to the center, rode on the thick butt which twitched like a jackstraw; and he remembered the stout hickory growing on the ridge he had cut to make the sweep. She was bounding down now, fair in the center, taking the rapids, riding atop as the falls opened to her and took her down, and she bounded like a lady in a waltz, glided down into the gentles where the river widened in a pool of light.

The men from the broadhorn, crews at the sweeps, gave them a Cock-a-doodle-do, flapping their hands against their sides. One bearded, broad-chested river roarer shouted, "Where you bound?"

"Bound clean down," Abe shouted.

"What's yore handle?"

"Abe—Abe Lincoln."

"Give Abe Lincoln and his little pardner there a long whoop and a holler and a trifle more." They had chests like buffaloes and they set the Ohio shores ringing. The vikings of the inland waters began to pull their big sweeps, roaring lustily, and Abe and Allen pulled their raft behind and rode in their wake singing too.

Row, boys, row
Down the O-hi-o
Gals down to Shawneetown
R'arin' fer to go.

Hard upon the beach oar!
She moves too slow
All the way to Shawneetown.
Row, boys, row.

So it was this way they rode safely past the white cliffs of Cave-in-the-Rock—the crowing old river roarers, bending to their sweeps, with a boy who was becoming a man, in a new nation, feeling his voice rounding and lowering as he bellowed in the wake of his countrymen.

When night fell they tied to a landing, one of the poor river settlements which described themselves by their names—Horse Tail Ripple, Sister Snags, Hog Hole, Sour Bears Eddy, Dead Man's End. Abe had learned now not to tie up to a high bank, or near a cave, but on a wide sweep of beach where you could see who was coming at you. Outlandish men, women, and children came down to see the broad-horn tie up, and the raft with the tall man and the little man.

They took hold of Allen, asking him to come to the dancing. Abe saw they were a tough crowd, and strode up and pulled Allen away, and they all began joshing him. "Who's yore tall friend? He's got a tall spire. Blow my whistle and ring my bell but he's a tall one . . . . A scarecrow must've plucked him out'n an Injianny cornfield."

Allen said, "Better not meddle with him. He's a sleeping tornado."

"Why," one of the river roarers strutted up, "cock-a-doodle-do. I can out-run, out-jump, out-swing, chew more 'baccy, spit further than anyone on the river or off it." He was thick, broad, square, squatty, and ox-strong, and Abe didn't feel like tangling with him. He was redtanned, bursting out of his pants and his skin, with fists like hams, and he looked bleached, tanned, burnt-cooked, smoked and salted by wind and water. His bare chest was big as a buffalo, sun-cured like smoked ham; and his bare feet took hold of the earth like claws; his grinders shone as if he bit nails to keep them in practice for biting off ears and noses. He wore a red feather out of his thicket of matted hair.

Abe had heard their fighting was free and fanciful with ear-chewing, neck-biting, kicking, butting, hair-pulling, and any other kind of make believe you could think of. He had heard a fight with them, whooping it up, bear traps, fur flying, and hammer claws was like a cornfield in fall—no ears left.

"I'm a peaceful man," Abe said, "and a tired one."

"Here, pardner, down the gullet!"

"I don't drink," Abe said.

"Ho, you don't insult me twice, refuse my fight, refuse my drink. I'll pour it down for you, pardner."

"Better leave him alone," Allen said. Abe stood slack and grinning as if there was no danger in him. The crowd was against him, but he aimed to drive in a wedge of jokes and swing an axe of good will, and lay them down on his side.

A tall, gaunt, wild-weathered woman, her hair tied in a buckskin, turned Abe around. "So you don't wet yore fodder, hey?"

"Watch out for her," another cried. "You'll go down like a squealing pig down an alligator gullet."

Abe grinned. "I got more luck with the river than with women."

"Air you a free-willed Methodist?" she said.

"Well," said Abe, "I'm a hickory sapling, plenty of give but hard to break."

The men made their first laugh and Abe knew he had got them.

"Go it, Oxblood," someone yelled.

Oxblood laughed. "I'm a highwater snagger myself, a snortin', snappin' turtle, a salt river roarer, born in a hurricane; I can tow a broadhorn with my teeth, let in an acre of sunshine in any wood; when I suck in my breath the rivers meet in the middle. I once stomped my feet and made a hole to China."

"Cock-a-doodle-do," the men cried, as Oxblood pranced up and down, put out his fists and made to take hold of the lean, lanky boy who seemed to be standing relaxed as he would on any summer evening. Suddenly he took hold of the river roarer. "You talk too much," Abe said, mowing him down with talk. "Your hurricane deck is on the small side; you got no power in yore paddles, nothing in the pilothouse; and you no doubt run on low pressure most of the time for you already blowed your bilers. I got steady steam and going power to glory."

There was a moment of shocked silence, then the crowd roared. Now he had them.

"Take out your pistols," Oxblood screamed, jumping in the air so his beard jarred and his hair stood on end. "Choose yore weapons, knives, axes, banana knives or bare knuckles. See if you can do this." And he pulled out his pistols, aimed at an Indian standing with the crowd. "I'll shoot off his scalp lock. Whar's the man can pluck hit?" And before Abe could stop him he had shot straight into the crowd, and shot off the scalp lock of the Indian, a dastardly piece of shooting.

Abe sprang at him, took hold and threw him down. Oxblood rose, roaring, bellowing, charged and they met head on—the big man trying to get a gouge hold, but Abe arched like a sapling, sprang out of his hold, and the giant searched for him like a blind man, with the crowd roaring. They sparred, glared, capered. Abe, wary as a cricket, broke his holds, kept out of his bear hug. The big man was heavy, earth-bound, but he could crush you like a bear or fell you like a tree. Abe, like a skinny cock, danced around him, and the crowd began to enjoy his skill and method, and roared. At last Abe got the headlock on him; snapped the big man into the air; flipped him over like a fish on a hook; and he hurtled through the air, and landed like an earthquake in the sand.

Abe stood amidst the cheers, relaxed, grinning—a tall, lanky scarecrow. The men in the butternut shirts crowded around him and shook his hand. "Upper river laid low down river man," they said. "My crow is always for the upper river man; lower river men the best," and several fights started over this. "This boy never been below before, why he's a bar and catamount combined."

They all squatted down to talk; somebody built a little fire, and it pleasured Abe as much as anything to be taken as brother to these old and new river men, full of talk, of grief and laughter, full of history—makers of history, bearers of burdens of time and work, making new territories, new children. He read them like he read the forests, the land. Their rugged, seamed, burnt, strong faces were pages telling of hardships, struggles, strains of deep melancholy and loneliness; and he read the building of a nation from the huge work hands, the kindled eye, the heartwood of man, the plain people in the long struggle carrying upon their shoulders the great and durable questions of all ages.

That night Abe laughed more than he ever had before. He stuck his fist through his coonskin hat, slapped his knees, doubled up, snapped back, slapped others on the back, laughed till he was sore. They squatted around the fire in their butternut jeans with knotted whangs, as they talked of places Abe had never seen, of factories in the east, of the new steam engine on rails, of spinning jennies that made cloth; some had been to far, far countries, and fought in many wars. They talked of the things they had built—bridges, buildings, the new Erie Canal; they told about the country north, of the Mandan Indians. He heard river lore—that there were three hundred and ninety crossings from shore to shore, bend to bend, which added five hundred miles; he heard of terrible storms, and river beasts. They were a brave, generous, jolly, rollicking set, rude, rough, full of truth and honesty and the wisdom of work.

The land sounds mingled with river sounds, with frogs, owls, or a fiddle from the bluff. Abe thought he would like to learn their talk and always be simple and real and true to the earth like these men. The talk turned to slavery and some had pieces of the jigsaw puzzle to contribute—they had been on slave ships and had their stomachs turned by what they saw. They didn't know the answer to it—some felt it was none of their business; others took fire like dry tinder.

Abe asked them if they were Jackson men, and a roar went up, and they said asking them that was like asking a hog if he liked mash. And Abe found himself, without his asking, the center around the fire, making a speech and as always making the men laugh a little, putting a wedge in, "I'm a long jackknife doubled up in the handle. The extreme point of the blade has to move through a wide space before it is open, but when the jackknife is open it cuts wide and deep. I am six foot and over, and it takes me a good while to open and shut. Or you might say I'm like a well-plaited, long, and heavy ox lash. A lash like that when swung around and around high in the air, on a good whip stalk, well seasoned, by an expert ox driver, and popped and cracked and snapped at a lazy ox shirking its duty, it cuts to the raw, brings blood, opens a gash, and makes the lazy ox sting with pain but makes him move—so you might say the lash flung through the air has set a force in action. Well, the slave lash is like that. And it falls on our backs."

At first he stood, awkward, rising into the darkness—a little ungainly, shy, and the men all smiled at each other; but as he spoke, something happened that people later were always to notice when Abe Lincoln spoke—his face filled out; his awkwardness turned to nobility; his squeaking voice rounded. As he always did later, he did now, ran his thumbs around each other, and lifted his bony finger to shake at his audience; and every man jack sitting there felt something of a curious miracle, saw a boy become a man, saw an awkwardness change into power. He extended his arms, clenched his bony, strong axe hands, his gray eyes flashed, and it seemed to him that on the frontier all was open, visible, clear and these men too were strong, open, and he stood on a level floor with them, open and clear to them, as they were open and clear to him. And he said to the night, to the men he loved, to the river that would see bloody battles, "Slavery must not stand against liberty, justice, and progress of all mankind . . . ."

These words like the fire seemed to warm the men and weld them together, as they saw that it must be so.

Around the bend, sparking the darkness, glowing her head off, came a stern-wheeler, the wet tinder striking fire, and music as well as smoke and sparks coming out of her. "Thar's progress," cried the men. The steamboat meant the death of them, and no more use for their skills. "Ain't she hummin'? Ain't she beautiful? There's progress fer you. Puts me out of a job. It's death to the old river ways, the rafters, the roarers. Watch her glide. You should see her come upstream, only a man who's brought her up with his naked back can know what it means." So they all spoke at once.

Long and narrow she sat, high and rakish and alight upon the night river. "Cricky," Abe said, as he saw the lighted boat, and the ladies and gentlemen in silks and breeches dancing the minuet, delicate and strange upon the river night. And then he saw what they all saw, for in the bowels of the boat, stoking her boilers, were black men and above the sound of paddle, the boilers, the minuet, came the sound of

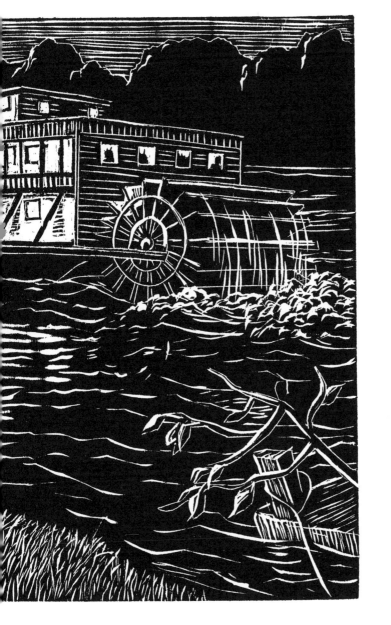

ankle chains. "There's why you can't get no job on those river boats. I'm agin' 'em. Man was invented fust. It ain't natural. I'm fer the natural man, sweep and pole, and the natural river."

One of them thrust out his boot and squelched the fire. The river boat took the light downriver and a sadness was in the night. Abe saw men whose jobs were gone. They knew their brawn, muscle, know-how, man sense, and manpower, was giving way to steam, a hundred horsepower, and the half-alligator, half-horse man would be gone, choked out like a bear from the hollow tree. Now they cut wood for the boilers but that would be gone when coal came in and the red-feather men would be gone, and their broad poles and the sweep, and their singing would be heard no more; their campfires cold, and the river would reflect old images on nights like this and new images of new power and struggle.

Abe said good-night to the stout river men, and went back to the raft where he sat for a long time, jackknifed over his knees, taking measurements of himself. Allen had gone to the bluff and the water lapped the raft gently, lipping strange presentiment of disaster which he had all his life—of some violent happening. But he held to these men he had known,

and told himself in all his thinking he would start
with their knowing, speak simply, and true to the
ways of their understanding.

CHAPTER 10

THE NEXT MORNING they cut cable, hallooed good-bye to their friends, and started downhill to New Orleans. Now Abe wanted to gab with all the people of the river, and when they tied up in the evening he took his needles, pins, and thimbles, went aboard, gathered scraps of news the like of which he had never heard before, got himself a poke of jokes, river sayings, songs and troubles, and felt the people made fiber in him as flax weaves to the cloth.

Every morning they started early in the summer sun floating into warmth. The country opened strange before them, dead timber swamps, crooked channels opening out into alligator and hurricane bars. They passed Shawneetown, where a mighty curve bore them straight west. They lost track of

100

time. One day they took off their buckskins, let the sun fall on them in February, and dived into the river, and warmed themselves naked on the raft. It didn't seem healthy or natural to them to be so warm in February. The air was warm, and on the shore they saw for the first time the giant live oaks standing in their mossy beards, with mistletoe green in the branches.

"It ain't America," Abe kept saying, as he sat at the bow reading out loud to himself. Every day now he got a newspaper from upriver, or downriver, and now, more and more, he got the New Orleans paper, and he was surprised to read a paper attacking Jackson, and with ads saying slaves for sale in it. He sat in the sun and let the raft drift, his legs wound around each other. Sometimes he draped himself over a barrel, the paper on the logs; and sometimes one leg would be in the water and the other high as the barrel. Allen was frightened when he saw Abe read. You could speak right at him and he wouldn't hear—such concentration would fell a possum right out of a tree. And he read out loud. When Allen asked him why, he said it was because he got the idea twice, to two senses, coming and going. "I remember it better. It's a hard thing to get an idea like splittin' logs. You got to swing the axe with a mighty stroke; there's knots of superstition all bound together. Old ideas are like old wood, they fight back. An idea is like a tree—took a century to grow it—it's against change, conservative by nature, and the axe is the radical—it's got to bite deep and hold, strike into the cleft, hold the cranium open and pour in a new thought, a wedge, until the old knots and old woods accept it, and all the little minds are jolted apart and lie open to reason."

Allen was pulling his whiskers out with a clam shell. "You might as well put that bar grease away, Allen Gentry," Abe lowed. "You ain't goin' to Natchez-under-the-Hill when and if we come to it. I'll have to shut you in like I did that mongrel of Pa's."

"No wonder he bit you," Allen said.

"We are going to slide right past that wicked place straight downhill to New Orleans and there I'll hog-tie you, Allen Gentry."

"I aim to have me a fling before I marry the girl my pa wants me to and settle down to be a farmer."

Abe unwound his legs, swung them in the air, swatted a big poisonous-looking fly and looked at the live oaks on the shore. There was something made him afraid—the air was too still; the sun was a round hot ball, the likes of which he had never seen. They passed Shoo-Fly Bar and Wolf Island and a mass of alligators, pulled up on the beach. Men and women who lived like animals along the fringe of forests were trying to keep cool. Abe thought he had never seen such squalor and wickedness. At night when they tied up, they heard screaming, and gambling, and killing.

By day, Abe saw, mile on mile, the bluffs and the big plantations above them, and below the squalid settlements and the shacks of the Negroes. He saw children planting and hoeing cotton, and sometimes he heard the strange singing not of free men but of slaves.

It was unnatural, heat like this, planting crops, the round sun at noon, the awful fragrance of plants and tropical fruits he did not know. He felt he was pointed like a bird dog toward some disaster.

At the wharves he saw gentlemen and ladies and their black servants. It seemed more like a European life he had heard men tell of, where men were serfs and there were rulers and kings. Allen often said, "Not so bad down here if you're on top. Look at the life they lead there on the bluffs. Pretty women, too. They say you can make a heap of money chasing runaway slaves, four or five hundred a head, give you capital."

"Would you sell a man?"

"Well a black man ain't the same. They're like children. Need us to take care of them."

"I wouldn't like to sell nary a man of any color. I don't know the rights of slavery in the South but I wouldn't sell nary a man."

"But a white man making a slave of a black man is a different thing."

"Well," Abe said, "it is color then, the lighter having the right to enslave the darker. Take care, Allen, there. You could be the slave of the first man you meet with a skin fairer than your own."

"By cricky," Allen said, struck by this logic. "The white man is superior."

"Ho ho, that's what you mean, heh? By this rule you could be the slave of the first man you might meet with an intellect superior to your own. So you say it's a question of interest, so then if you can make it your interest to enslave another, why they can make it their interest to enslave you? Ain't that right now? If men are to be property, then pretty soon all men will go back to being property like they was in the old country, and we'll be back whar we started from."

"You shore make a case, Abe." Allen said.

"Well," said Abe, "it's hard to figure the right of it. A slave now is property worth to some white men—hundreds of dollars. A slave must be worth five hundred to a thousand dollars a piece or more, think of that."

"It's sure as sin nobody'd give that much fer us, eh Abe?"

"Well, there's a point to ponder on now, if a man becomes something besides a human being—that is property, not a person but a thing—it changes everything. If you break down the idea that man is free and equal, each man himself, then it won't be long before they will begin to make things of the poor white man too. It's bound to happen. You can't have democracy while one man is a slave; that's clear in my mind as a hickory knot."

As they floated down, Abe thought of slavery, and the red sun drove before them and went down beyond the southern swamps. And the knotty problem stood before the axe of his mind. Was slavery his own problem? Did it affect every man—or could you say you were not your black brother's keeper?

Could a democracy exist half slave and half free men? It would be a long time before he and the nation would find any answers.

That night he woke, Allen shaking him. "What's the matter?" Abe leaped up in all his clothes, laying about him with the axe handle he had been smoothing off.

Allen said, "You were yelling 'half slave and half free.' I thought you were going to kick the salt off the top of my head, Abe. For Heaven's sake go to sleep, Abe Linkern."

The raft hardly moved. The air, the water were becalmed. The current itself seemed to have stopped. You couldn't breathe. Abe felt his stomach churn as he looked at the red, smoky ball that had been the sun. They had to pole through the thick air and it seemed the sky was upon them. Men and women fanned themselves on the cabin roofs, and the cats and chickens huddled like ghosts and the smoke didn't ride the air, hung dead, becalmed.

Then Abe saw a green light rise in the wind, and a jagged green lightning; and suddenly the trees began to rock at the tops in a crazy way. The river began to run on its surface, come alive, and then to roar and heave. Abe and Allen began frantically to pole to shore, but they were caught and whirled around like a chip. A huge hand scooped them up as the river seemed to turn and flow back uphill. The cliffs and the woods seemed turned on end, and the raft was whirled around and around as the water seemed to leave the river bed. Abe wondered if Allen had been swept away. Then the raft seemed to float on water of brass, and Abe began to hold her to the stream again. Then she scudded into light; the air lifted; the wind was gone, and he smelled a sweet odor of rain and crushed foliage and his own drenched skin, and he saw Allen tied to the cabin. He had wound the cable around his body.

"Now I got you permanent," Abe grinned.

"Get me out, I'm choking from the chain."

The boats began to float down the channel again. A big broadhorn was wrecked. Someone shouted that a child had been swept overboard, men were wading with hooks and ropes, searching for bodies.

Abe felt shaken as if he had seen some devil of nature, some witchcraft from the old bearded oaks, from the strange southern land, alien to him, with some danger in it he could only sense but not name.

CHAPTER 11

NOW THEY ENTERED the Nine Mile Stretch. Natchez was a hundred and seventy miles down. New Orleans three hundred further. Allen was washing his clothes, slicking up, saying he was surely now a man on his own, while Abe said he was surely going to take him back to his pa at Gentryville all in one piece.

"Look at my muscles," Allen said, flexing his skinny arm.

"Surely looks like you got bean pods under yore skin," Abe laughed.

One evening they came neck and neck with a raft with a paddle wheel. Horses turned a mill wheel in the center, which turned the paddle wheel, and drove the raft at a swift pace up and down the river.

On it was a splendid-looking man with a flowing beard. He had a strong, hearty wife with beautiful braids round her head thick as flax, and Abe couldn't count the golden and laughing children that played under the flapping wash hung out on lines to dry. There was even a little garden on one end of the raft, and a cabin like a real house with little windows and curtains and flowers blooming.

"Air you an inventor?" Abe shouted to them, as they tied up at Hurricane Bend, and the man laughed a hearty laugh. "Inventions someday will take care of all labor. I can lick the current back without black or white slave, sir. These nags will bring me back slicker'n a mud turtle climbing up a wet bank. I'll breast back again and ask no favor of half-horse or half-alligator men, or slaves in chains."

That night Allen slicked up and went to dance with the gals at a little cabin where the fiddler seemed about to burst the seams. Abe's raft rocked gently beside the broadhorn. The patriarch had put his horses out to graze on a little plateau. The night was strange and alien, and Abe felt lonely and homesick. A soft little mist wandered like a little gray cat over the surface of the river—or was it like seeing a dim figure in his memory that came and went. He closed his eyes and remembered how he and his ma played hide-and-seek, and blindfolded he felt for her and found her, and she would whirl him up in her bread-smelling hands and toss him in the air. He thought she just turned the bend of the river with the little whiffs of heat mist. He felt fear, and time, and the night, and all things that were lost, the seasons before he himself was born, marked by blaze trails of men whose campfires had long gone out. He had cut himself tree marks on lost trails, still bent to mark the lost trails of Indians. He had laid his axe to the deep root of trees growing secret and strong like himself—ages stored in them as in him— and now time, the river, the night laid its axe deep in his own heart.

He couldn't bear to sit there, and he heard laughter from the broadhorn, and a woman singing, so he took his kit and went to see if he could sell them some needles, or a knife, or a thimble to take the place of a lost one. He walked past the raft and saw the last light strike the woman who sat with a baby on her knees. She looked at him and he felt all legs, and folded his long arms behind him, grabbing his elbows with his fingers. One of the children laughed and he thought it might be at him. And his sadness deepened, and all his old awkwardness came into him, and a feeling of something being amiss.

A great dog leaped out at him, barking, and the children screamed. The woman said severely, "Down, Jackson, down." And the father and husband strode out and his voice cowed the hound.

"Jackson?" Abe said. "Andy Jackson?"

The woman laughed, and now they were all looking at him. "We call him that because he chases the money lenders and collectors away."

"I'm a Jackson man myself," Abe said. "Please to relay that message to your hound. Reminds me of the story of the man who killed a dog with a pitchfork because the dog attacked him. 'What made you kill my dog with your pitchfork?' the owner asked. 'What made him try to bite me?' the man said. The owner said, 'Why didn't you go at him with the other end of the pitchfork?' The man attacked said, 'Why didn't he come after me with the other end of the dog?' "

Abe felt warmed when they all laughed, most heartily, and the littlest children tangled themselves around his legs. He was invited in and given a glass of cider, and he showed them his water trick. He was as full of fun as a dog has fleas. He put the glass of cider between his heels, folded his arms, bent his tall form backward until he could grip the edge of the cup between his teeth, then straightened himself up without spilling the cider. The children all laughed and hugged his knees. "Back up and spread out yore arms, and stand solid on yore feet, no stretchin', and see how tall ye air."

"Well," said Mr. Todd, "if'n a tall man can see over the horizon you'd be apt to be that man to see into the future for us and see if it's the honey bee and not the wolf is goin' to have us."

Mrs. Todd bought some needles and told him they were from Massachusetts, and he asked many questions about that country. He remembered the tales his pa told about the aristocrats, the Tories, who shot at the soldiers from their windows as they marched by; of Hananian Lincoln, a first cousin, who fought at Brandywine under Washington; and another cousin, Amos, from Massachusetts, who was one of the men, his family said, who rigged themselves up as Indians and dumped the taxed tea into the Boston Harbor from the British ship, to show their disobedience and contempt for taxation without representation. They had come through that gap down Wilderness Road and now these had come through another gap, the Ohio River—down another road.

"We keep a moverin'," Father Todd said. "Why it's told in my family they moved so much 'round the country that every time the chickens heard the sound of wagon wheels they laid down with their legs crossed waiting to be tied!" Abe laughed heartily even though he had heard the story, and told some himself and hoped they would give him the same courtesy of laughter.

Mr. Todd told how his Dutch family had been driven off their land by English landlords, put on such rack rents they could not pay. But they had fought back, had penny sales, stuck on their land, blowing tin horns to call the other farmers when a sheriff came to put them off.

Abe looked at this man and woman, father and mother of six sons, five daughters, and he saw the wonderful calmness and strength in them all and the health of their skin and the hair of many colors and the long beard of the father, and the richness of his manners; the strong full beauty of the mother, with her golden braids around her head. You would wish to sit long with these people of the earth and know their wisdom. He could see the strong hands sowing, reaping, threshing, kneading bread.

"And," Father Todd was saying, "they lived in the rich houses and we got poorer and poorer like slaves." So there it was again, the question of slaves. "Some earn their bread by the sweat of their brow." Mr. Todd was something of a preacher. "And others toil not, neither do they spin. It is the effort of some to shift the share of the common labor to the shoulders of others. It is the durable curse of man."

Then Mrs. Todd told how they had hidden a Negro woman and her baby, and the question of slavery came up as it always did in any talk, north or south, east or west. And Abe lay before them his questions. All the arguments of Mr. Breckenridge he lay out as his own, to trap them into giving him leads and traces so he could prove and demonstrate the right of it. He said maybe it would be better to let the South keep their slaves; maybe each new state should vote the right and wrong of it—and this was like lighting a match to dynamite. Mr. Todd rose and strode up and down, pointing his finger at Abe's nose.

"Young man," he spoke in a thundering open-air voice which he must have used before. "You know not whereof you speak. Wrong cannot be voted in. Have we come this far from Tom Paine and Jefferson? We must not submit to anything wrong. Young man, ask nothing but what is right."

He went on and nothing could stop him when Abe said, "But some of the principal citizens seem to be for slavery."

"Principal citizens—there are no principal citizens. Every man in America is a principal citizen, including slaves. Yes that's what we fought for at Valley Forge. Now you're an odd, singular, and graceful man; you represent a new man. I can see your time and your age. We raise up here men to represent us—not a special man nurtured in ease and luxury, but the men of the river, and the settlements, men like you and me, and women like that, and children like that—the common man and woman of the swamps and the brakes, the rivers and prairies, and we will knit our generation together; speak to all generations of man; wipe out this terrible crime of slavery, and the little foxes in our vineyard. We who have fought the lion down shall not give in now to indignity to any man."

And Abe saw how the little foxes of compromise had gnawed at his own vineyard, and how here was a breed like his own who would die for the right and take nothing less; who could not be bought by little hucksters; who stood at every battle, and would stand in us all.

This man set him free of Mr. Breckenridge and the smart talkers and the jackals in the hen roost.

"You read this," Mr. Todd said, and gave him the first Abolitionist paper he had ever seen. The abolition of slavery—that was it, plain and simple, and there were men somewhere for that.

Then they heard a strange sound—a rhythmical kind of beat. One voice seemed to cry out, from the very earth itself came this strange moan; then the clank and strike of metal. Then it was repeated exactly as it came nearer.

Their eyes had grown used to the night and the shimmer of starlight and its reflection in a quiet river, so they saw etched in darkness around the bend a stream of monster flatboats coming upriver, and being pulled from the shore by a file of black slaves whose shoulders bent to the ground as, with each moan, they bit into the weight together, pulled it forward a foot. On the raft itself, like dancers on the end of long poles, were other slaves, bent along her hulls, bending on the gunwales almost horizontal to the water as they shoved her in rhythm with the men on shore. On the cabin roof, timing the set-ting-pole men with the men on shore, were two men who cried out, "Set pole—lift pole—and PULL." The men along the gunwales and the men on shore pulled together to the shout, "Send her snorting, bullies!"

Abe and Mr. Todd and the children looked at each other and then away. Mr. Todd lifted his mighty arms like Isaiah in the Bible. He cried out against evil, "A curse on all wealth piled by bonds-men. Every drop of blood drawn with the lash shall be paid for by the sword; the slave will rise and stand with freemen."

The boat would have to inch toward them, then past them, then up the river. Abe could not stand to stay with his friends all that time. Their warmth and talk now would be stricken every moment with that terrible ritual—"Send her snorting—set pole—place pole. Let her go!" And then the pull, and that dread-ful burden slowly creeping northward.

He left them a sharp, long hog knife, and a thim-ble for Mrs. Todd, and bid them goodnight, taking the Abolitionist paper in his pocket.

He didn't sleep much that night. Allen came late. The next morning the river where the slaves had pulled the barges left no trace now. Mrs. Todd was hanging out wash. The fair children were playing and bathing and laughing. The horses were ready, and Mr. Todd had to push his boat out himself, running from the boat's bow, the raft flowing away under his feet, and race to the rear and plant his pole again, bend, walk the gunwale, step to the bow, and shove her along to mid-channel by himself, with bend of back, and heft, and heave, and sweat, and man willingness, until his horses could get the turn of the mill wheel deep in the channel. He would be in New Orleans long before they would.

"Abolitionist," Abe thought, as he waved to them. "I'll see you again."

CHAPTER 12

IT WAS ABE'S birthday the night he was almost killed.

Allen was in a huff because they had passed Natchez-under-the-Hill during the storm and saw in the mist only a dirty cluster of shacks, gambling flats, and barges. Below Natchez the country flattened; the wide, empty land smoked in unhealthy mists; the turtles got bigger, the sun hotter. They floated by the dens of vice, hugged the banks at night; by day they passed groves of oranges, magnolias, and the great white houses on the bluffs and below on the docks Negro slaves sweated, and sang, pulling the produce boats up from New Orleans. They saw, too, the poor whites in the squalid villages, and the shacks of the Negroes, and they seemed to hold on their naked shoulders the big white plantations.

Abe wanted only to get to New Orleans, sell the produce, perhaps ship out on a cargo boat, or get a job in one of the tobacco fields, get the feel of how land and people were treated in this strange country.

Allen wanted to stop that night, but Abe wanted to go on. The tide now seemed to grip them strongly and carry them down. The night was heavy and sweet, a kind he had never known in the north, and he sat on the deck, the sweep lazily against his shoulder in case they met a boat. Feeling sleep coming on—he saw Allen already sprawled asleep—he gently let the raft swing into a cove, saw it was well anchored against a fallen tree, and let the raft rock him to sleep.

Suddenly he woke, standing upright. He had heard a scream, the sound of naked feet running and felt the shock of the raft tipping with extra weight. He stood blind for a moment not knowing where he was, then he heard it again—Allen screaming. He picked up his hickory axe handle and ran across the tipping raft and he saw Allen down, his arms upraised against the shadows of a number of men who seemed to be striking him. Abe let out a scream and dove into the huge shadows of the men belaying about him. He drove them before him.

But he was pinioned from behind by three more who for a moment held his arms. The ones he had driven away turned back upon him. He turned quickly, broke loose, backed against the small cabin and still with his hickory stick he began to drive them toward the dark shore.

The next few minutes he could never remember, only that he was fighting for his life, in a kind of battle he had never fought before.

It seemed quiet. He heard his stick swish and fall on flesh. He struck one from behind and heard him go howling toward shore, swimming in the water. Another dove off. A third and another sprang on him and with his foot he kicked one to the deck, and he struck the other with his fist. Another must have run. He felt himself struck on the head and must have for a moment gone out, but he came to with his arms around the broad shoulders of the most powerful and desperate man he had ever touched.

It was then that he knew this was a different kind of fight than he had ever fought before. These men wanted to kill him, not for food, but because they hated him, with a bitter, terrible hatred. This man struck at him, gripped him in a rock-like and awful grip so he thought they would both go down to the bottom of the river together. He felt the man had only one intention—to destroy him, to strike him down. He felt come from this powerful fighter the most awful hatred he had ever felt.

Trying every trick to free himself from the awful grip, he pushed the face back with his hand, feeling to gouge the eyes, and he saw that the man's face was black and he was looking into the most fearsome eye, alive with hate. Then he saw that the whole naked, sweating torso was black. He thrust all his weight in a blow against the black man and felt the black body fall from his hands, and for a moment he looked again into the eyes of the black man, as he lay upon the darkness for a moment, falling back away from him, his arms outstretched, his mouth open, his eyes in horror as he fell back into the water.

Abe tottered from the blow, blood blinding his eyes, and he felt an anxiety for the man, knowing he would be unconscious and perhaps drown. Shaking he stood, his bloody head hanging down. He did not hear the Negro surface or swim on, and he felt a terrible relationship with this unknown fighter, still felt his awful power in his hands, against him, and saw the dark face falling, as in a dream, into the water.

But just then he heard Allen shout, "Are you all right, Abe? Where are you, Abe? Abe. Abraham Linkern."

Abe wanted only to get away from the shore, away from those seven black men, for now in his memory he saw that they all had been black, runaway slaves perhaps wanting some of their store of bacon and flour. But they had struck him in mortal hatred. They had wanted above all to kill him. What had he done to them that made them want to kill him? Frantically he took the sweep and poled out to mid-stream and saw the shore where they had disappeared fade away.

Allen had no mark on him but he was screaming and shouting the most awful curses, and jumping up and down and shaking his fist. "Seven black giants, goin' to git our stores, goin' to kill us."

"They aimed to kill us, that's for sartin," Abe said. "They wanted to kill us."

"They wanted to steal our raft and our stores."

"Maybe they was hongry. They fought like we was mortal enemies. I never fought a man who hated me like that. I think I'm goin' to be sick."

"Why, Abe, yore bleedin'. Yore hurt. They busted in yore head." Allen wet his shirt and bathed Abe's eye, a deep cut, bleeding badly.

"I wonder if that one got to shore safe," but he really wondered why he had not jumped in after him as he would have done for any man.

Allen was excited with a curious hatred. "Those damn black slaves, no better than animals."

"They fight better," Abe said. "I never see a better fighter than that one. They wanted most to kill us. Why?"

"Black apes," Allen said, and he was shaking.

"Maybe they were escaping from those chains, from their masters. From their slavery."

"Oh, they don't mind it, they're like children."

"That was no child had hold of me. We were almost killed, not by men merely trying to rob us, but by something which gripped us both in a terrible force. I thought we were going to kill each other. I wanted to kill him. I thought we would both go to the bottom of the river in this awful deadlock. I am not his master, his enslaver. Why did he hate me?"

After winning a good fight you usually felt splendid, but Abe felt as if something had been taken from him he could not name—as if he had been in some nightmare and he knew that all his life he would feel the magnificent body of that man; see for a moment the flash of communication from the eyes; see the man lying upon the dark, going down in pain, terror, bravery, and revenge.

"They're not men," Allen chattered.

"They're men," Abe said fiercely. "I was the one who fought like a beast. I wanted to kill him too.

"Black slaves ain't men. They're made different."

"They had faces, bodies, parts of men; they cried, they bled, and perhaps that one died."

Abe leaned over the raft edge and was violently sick; and the scar he would wear all his life opened again and bled.

CHAPTER 13

THEY WERE ENTERING the great deltas and you had to be half-alligator and half-horse, sometimes getting out to push from the shore, to take the raft through myriad boats, pirogues, steamboats, shouting peddlers, fishermen, cursing boatmen shouting in every language under the sun. Allen and Abe had not had a night's sleep since the fight. They had been afraid to tie up at night, had spelled each other, kept the raft moving through the crisscross river, around sharp points, into broad delta land where it was hard to find the river channel. Abe felt he would never be the same again.

When he dozed off he found himself running through dense forests, down lost traces with hound dogs after him; he would think he was the hunter,

126

and then in a cold sweat he would find he was the hunted. Once, as he was being pursued, he leaned over a glassy stream and saw he wore his own face but it was black, and then he fell backward into the water. Once he dreamed he was fighting and both the fighters were himself, one with a white face, one with a black. Then he would dream he was a beast laying about him to kill seven hungry men.

The mosquitoes bit him, and the heat was cloying. He gave up sleeping and poling and tried to find out the rights of this awful thing—drive a wedge into it somewhere. He had guiding lights and whispers and sometimes shouts—his people and his church had always been against slaves. His pa had given up the best paying job he ever had because he would not arrest fleeing slaves hunting their freedom. The Hankses and the Lincolns, the plain and commonality he had known, had fought against white slavery of every kind, for "All men are created equal." Had they meant it? His grandfather at King's Mountain had meant it. The dignity of the common man, his work, his life had always been real in the common people of his kind.

He didn't want to stop at the wharves; talk to the people. He sat silent, tried to read the signs of the great plantations, with their white pillars, marks of leisure and comfort, and the caves, taverns, squalid settlements below like a sign and signal of some split—up and down—north and south. This was a trace he had never followed and he knew he read signs of sickness and death. It was a different thing to argufy about it in Pigeon Creek. It was a live, dangerous thing and could kill you, and what was more could kill an idea, a belief.

Then they saw the tall masts at the wharves of New Orleans, the levees where the big ships were from foreign lands, the sun-flecked pilings.

They had to pole through a wharf river town of rafts, peddlers, women hanging their wash on rafts, fires burning, a hum of bees. They stood and gawked at the sights they had never seen. People shouted at them, bunted them, yelled in strange languages, laughed; some women threw flowers on them, making them blush; flags waved; the sun shook everything in a hot, splendid light.

They jockeyed into the wooden levee, hailed Mr. Todd who waved from a huge meal he was eating, a white rag around his beard, his horses nibbling the hats of women vendors. He helped them cable their raft; said he would look after it while they saw the town. He was himself waiting for the produce men to look at his load. Abe looked at the wharves loaded with cotton, pelts, hides, tobacco, hemp, and the warehouses that rose on the wharf, and the bargaining going on, and women vendors in bright turbans; and Abe looked away when he saw their faces were dark. He sweated with an awful guilt.

For he saw that every bale, barrel, and burden was carried on the head and shoulders of black slaves. They ran up the gangways and down again. They moved along the wharves chained together, pacing their movement by their sorrowful song. Gentlemen alighted from their carriages helped by Negro servants who held parasols over them, held their horses, came to heel like dogs. Abe had never seen a man a slave to another in this way. A crowd of people were laughing, and Abe could see over their heads—a Negro boy who wore a red cap like a monkey and was on a tether, and was scratching himself and aping, sitting on his master's trunk, and the crowd of white people were laughing. Abe looked away. Negro women with their babies were beating their clothes along the levee and Abe looked away when they raised their heads to look at him.

They had just started up the street from the levee, Allen looking like a New Orleans dandy already, when down the hill came a chain gang of Negroes, moving to their own chant, pulling along their ankles heavy balls. A bearded driver, a big white man, waved a rawhide snake whip, and snapped it around their bare chests as he barked at them like a maniacal dog. Again Abe found himself looking into the black face of a slave, and again felt the quick flash of intelligence, the recognition of his accusation and at the same time of his brotherhood. The blow on his head began to beat, and he put his hand to it, feeling sick and dizzy.

They walked up the narrow streets, peering into flowery courtyards where ladies sat, and into lacy iron balconies. They passed flower markets and the busy trade of a city the likes of which Abe had never dreamed. They rose into the rich streets and again Abe saw, above the squalor, the barter, the blood on the cobblestones, the rich leisure of a few. Who were they? Their grandfathers had not fought at Kings Mountain, had they? Or at Valley Forge. Had they?

But it was as if the bright sunshine, the flowers, the strange languages had a deep, a terrible shadow that darkened it all, and Abe began to see only the black faces, following the white men, with no place in the sun. He looked down when he met them. Once a Negro stepped off the sidewalk, and Allen had to grab Abe's arm again. "Yore crazy Abe. Forget it. Didja ever see anything like this boy? Don't get mixed up."

"We'll get mixed up with this, one way or another," Abe said, and he saw that there was a whole part of the city he could not speak to. If he spoke would they answer? Who were they? A Negro who looked like himself, a country man, a man of the land, was coming toward him. Abe held out his hand, spoke, "Brother you look like a farmer like myself." The man stopped as if he had held a dagger to him, bowed low, took a complete circle around him murmuring, "Yes sir, boss . . . . Yes sir, Mr. Boss . . . . Yes sir . . . ." Abe stood with his hand out, feeling blunted, diminished as a man, as part of this. He was no boss, never wanted to be a boss, neither did he want to be a servant. He followed Allen who was strutting like a young cock in a new hen roost. Girls waved to him. Abe held onto him reminding him they had still to sell their cargo.

Later in the day Abe saw people hurrying into a white-pillared, gleaming building. He had seen pictures of such buildings in glimpses into books. He had some impression that it represented an old society—Greek, he thought. He wanted to go into such a building, which seemed to him to represent some dignified human achievement of men long gone. Inside they entered a large, circular room with a high dome, and glass chandeliers, and gilt cupids. There were alcoves where famous white people's busts stood. There were groups of elegant gentlemen, ruffled, perfumed. Abe and Allen saw some of these gentlemen put their lace kerchiefs to their noses as they passed through.

Abe stood transfixed, unable to believe the reality of what he saw. For on a raised stand stood an auctioneer, and along the arena men with snake whips trotted Negro slaves up and down like cattle to test their wind and strength. Slave buyers from the plantations were buying men and women to work the fields of sugar and cotton and tobacco.

The auctioneer joked—"Gentlemen, we have the best stock bred in Virginia. You know what that means, black boys bred to the stables, a valuable mother and her three kids—we'll separate and sell them separate; and look at this strong girl—." Abe sickened as he saw the girl jerked onto the huge block, raised above the bidders. His head hurt; and suddenly he knew why he had been struck and almost killed.

The people being sold were black, and the people buying and selling them were white. *And he, Abe Lincoln, had a white face.* Now he knew why the slave wanted to kill him; why he had been locked in mortal combat with him—for he, Abe Lincoln, bore the white face of the plantation and bore the guilt. I tore the child from the mother. I put the bloody ball and chain upon the ankle. I worked him in the field, brought him over like a rat in the holds of a slave ship. It was I.

He did not know he was hauling Allen out of the place; that he was saying over and over, "I have a white face."

Allen was saying, "But you ain't got any slaves, Abe."

"We all have slaves in America—if even one man is a slave, and one man sits by and says nothing—there is guilt."

"They tried to kill us," Allen said, trying to keep up with the swift striding man.

"How many have we killed? We have white faces. We are their owners. That's what he saw on the raft—a white face—that's all. I saw a black face . . . ."

"I wouldn't mind ownin' slaves—" Allen started to say.

But Abe turned on him, took him by the collar, shook him like a rabbit. "I wouldn't be a slave and I wouldn't be a master."

"What air you gonna do?" Allen chattered, putting his collar back in place.

"We're gonna hit this slavery hard sometime if we get a chance. Now we're gonna sell our produce and get the next boat back up the river."

"Not me," Allen said.

"Yes, you," Abe said, "I told yore pa I'd bring you back and I'm goin' to bring you back."

"You said you was goin' to get yoreself a job and stay here."

"I'm goin' back to my people. I got work to do. I'm goin' back to Sarah—my mother—and her troubles, I'm goin' back to Indianny. I'm goin' home."

CHAPTER 14

THE NEXT DAY they sold their potatoes, bacon, flour, apples. Mr. Todd bought the raft for repairs on his boat and Abe gave Allen one day to see New Orleans. Abe walked alone down the streets; saw again the upper hills where the great white houses stood, and below the markets filled with the people—farmers, rivermen, carpenters, sailors, squatters. The talk he heard came back always to him, to set a measure all his life for the hard common sense and strength of the people, the builders, growers, planters, reapers, because they had in their hands the plow, the axe, the awl, the wheels, the shovel, and the steam, and always bore on their backs, and lifted with their arms, the burdens. He wanted then always to speak with no sham or lie to his countrymen, with

135

no dark-of-the-moon mystery; to demonstrate in the real, without shooting too high or aiming too low; to speak always to those who would understand him—the lifters, the bearers, the diggers, the plowers, the earth bearers, and workers.

They booked passage upstream on a steamboat, and Abe felt as they went back up the sugar coast, past the place where the storm had struck, where he had almost been killed by seven slaves, where his long thoughts and deep distress still seemed to possess his heart, that he had changed. He was a different person; his life would flow like a river blasted at its source, flowing a different direction to the sea.

He knew now that he was part of his country—of its paths, trees, man, woman, animal, great beasts and the tiny deer. He knew a man who becomes part of his people, of animals, land, cannot be discouraged or destroyed. Such a man, because he is not only himself and his own climbing or getting ahead, has in him the sorrow and tenderness, the tough fiber and sinew, the swing of the axe, the strength of the blacksmith, and the endurance of the mother. To destroy such a man or his memory you would have to destroy all the animals, erode all the land, turn back all the rivers, and the everlasting memory of the struggles of his people which could not be destroyed. First you would have to shut their mouths, dry up their brains, blast out their hearts.

And once they knew the right of slavery they would be a dangerous foe. Could a country have this property in men south of the Ohio, and north of that say, "All men are created equal"? He felt this was a tough, knotty, resisting problem forming that made him afraid. He knew how deeply wedged and grown in was the idea among his people, of men like his grandfather, Abraham, forming deep heartwood of hickory, of the equal man, who tipped his hat to nobody, the new forest prairie man, yes, the new man and woman at the spinning jennies, and crowded in the cities and those in the New Orleans market place. He saw men like himself, formed like himself, in the great common genus and principle, standing tall and bearing and generating within themselves a new labor, new strengths to strike at every form of despotism and slavery.

Sometimes his thoughts made him rise and stride around the deck, and men and women nudged each other. Some laughed, and some looked fearfully at him. So on the horizons of a country, a boy becomes a man in any time.

He said to Allen, as they leaned over the rail in the evening, that he did not want to become famous like Mr. Breckenridge, or a big lawyer. He told Allen that he had never been up and he didn't want to be higher than anyone. He said he would be with his people.

Allen said that nobody could put you down if you've never been up.

"Our land's in trouble, Allen Gentry," he said, making a circle in the air with his bony finger—a gesture historians would record later. "You won't be able to win enough hands of poker to keep you out of it."

"Money'll get you in and out of everything," Allen said, and went back to his game.

So this is the story of a few months in the life of a boy in the middle country becoming a man—when the sapwood of youth darkened, toughened, under strain and pressure, was fired, made stout and hickory-yielding. Men and nations are made by the firing of such days in their lives.

Such a knowing strengthens our own heartwood.

His loneliness and strength become our own.

Much of his history you know, but you can always as you grow have more knowing, see this great live oak of our history more clearly. You know he got back to Gentryville and that spring whipped down a little forest to build Sarah Bush a house, but the lumber was sold to Josiah Crawford and he cut more trees for his pa to make wagon wheels and axles; and all thirteen of them set out for the Sangamon in Illinois, an Indian name meaning the land of plenty. His pa sold his land, after fourteen years of improving it, clearing and plowing for Mr. Grigsby, for one hundred and twenty-five dollars cash. He had paid in the beginning two dollars an acre for the eight acres.

As you probably know, they packed their belongings, took the animals, seven yoke team of steer, and set out for a western land. Abe went again and lay in the dry winter grass and frozen wild vine and dogwood and said good-bye to Nancy Hanks. Naked they had come to the wilderness, and after toil, birth, death, building, planting, laughing, and weeping, they were leaving, naked as they had come.

The oxen and the train of wagons moved into long levels and ground swells of the Grand Prairie, with domes of sky and grass as tall as Abe. There he

cut down more trees and in Illinois, on the Sangamon, he raised a new cabin; made a new beginning
in a new country.

You know how he became President of the United
States, how he believed in the Union and carried
around in his tall hat the Emancipation Proclama-
tion which said:

*—that on the first day of January, in the year
of our Lord, one thousand eight hundred and
sixty-three, all persons held as slaves within any
state . . . the people whereof shall then be in
rebellion against the United States, shall be
then, thenceforward and forever, free.*

He became Father Abraham to us all, old Abe
Lincoln who believed we could read from darkness,
and build from shadows; son of the lonely Nancy
Hanks and of the great middle river and the heartwood of America.

And the long light falls upon us and as Abe's old
friend Herndon said, writing with an oil lamp in an
Illinois farmhouse, Abe was of those that "lean like
grand gray old towers, with lights on their brows,
almost dipping in the deep, the unknown, the

unknowable and unfathomable deeps of the future.
We thus come and go; in the coming and the going
we have moved forward."

MERIDEL LE SUEUR was born in Murray, Iowa, in 1900 and has spent most of her life in the Midwest. Her father was the first socialist mayor of Minot, North Dakota; her mother ran for Senator at age 70. After studying at the Academy of Dramatic Art in New York, the only job she could find was as a stunt artist in Hollywood. Her writing career began in 1928 when the populist and worker groups were re-emerging. While writing stories in the early thirties, which gained her a national reputation, she reported on strikes, unemployment frays, breadlines, and the plight of the farmers in the Midwest. She was on the staff of the *New Masses* and wrote for *The Daily Worker*, *The American Mercury*, *The Partisan Review*, *The Nation*, *Scribner's Magazine*, and other journals. Acclaimed as a major writer in the thirties, she was blacklisted during the McCarthy years as a radical from a family of radicals. Among her many published works are *North Star Country*, *Crusaders*, *Corn Village*, *Salute to Spring*, *Rites of Ancient Ripening*, *The Girl*, and *Ripening: Selected Work, 1927–1980*. The books for children by Le Sueur include *The Mound Builders*, *Conquistadores*, *The River Road: A Story of Abraham Lincoln*, *Chanticleer of Wilderness Road*, *Sparrow Hawk*, *Nancy Hanks of Widerness Road: A Story of*

Abraham Lincoln's Mother, and *Little Brother of the Wilderness: The Story of Johnny Appleseed*. Recent and forthcoming publications include *Winter Prairie Woman*, *Harvest Songs* (for which she received an American Book Award), and *The Dread Road* (a novel) to be published in 1991 by West End Press. She currently lives in Hudson, Wisconsin.

A native of the Midwest, SUSAN KIEFER HUGHES was born and raised in Kansas City, Missouri. She moved to California in her late twenties and directed a day care center for several years. Her enjoyment of children's books led her to the California College of Arts of Crafts in Oakland where she received her B.F.A. in Printmaking and fell in love with cutting wood. Her fine art books have been shown in the Victoria and Albert Museum in London, and are included in the collections of the Chicago Art Institute and the Library of Congress in Washington. Susan lives in Menlo Park with her two children, her press, and two inquisitive cats.